M,

Mercy

SHAYNE WOODSMITH

To Claire,

Thanks for all your support.

Cover illustrated by Christian Whitty

SHAYNE WOODSMITH
writes, makes movies, and takes photos. His fast-paced, thought-provoking, and at times utterly frantic, debut novel, *Twenty-Seven*, delivers a disarmingly honest portrayal of human frailty and strength while presciently casting a cold eye on our health-obsessed future. He is currently working on a collection of short stories and collaborating with Christian Whitty, the illustrator of this book's exterior, on a graphic novel. Most recently he has been compiling the stories and portraits of the inhabitants of Edmonton, Alberta, Canada with his Faces of Edmonton project. He lives in Edmonton with his spouse Megan and their two cats, Mortimer and Tuna.

Special thanks to Monique Pahud, Thomas Wharton, and Patti Wood. This is a better story because of you.

For Troy

Chapter 1

Surrounded by travellers and waddling like a penguin in a colony heading for open water, I inched closer to the security officers who looked like predators ready to pounce. I glanced into the eyes of every officer, dreading a scrutinizing gaze that lingered longer than normal.

I was next in line for the baggage scanner, metal detector, and potentially, a full-body digital strip search. The sixty-something man, a few people ahead of me, was going through a virtual pat down and body cavity search while forced to strike a put-your-hands-above-your-head-and-spread-'em pose inside of something that looked like a teleporter. I kicked off my shoes, slipped out of my belt, and emptied my pockets into a plastic bin. When it was my turn, an officer at the end of the security gauntlet moved his gaze back and forth between me and the clipboard he held in front of him.

He has a picture of me on it. Probably my fucking high school graduation photo, which would explain the double, triple, quadruple takes. DETAIN ON SIGHT stamped in red across my robe. Good thing nobody looks like their grad picture ten years later.

My duffle bag went into another bin and then everything I owned, save the clothes I wore, disappeared into a scanner. For a moment, I feared I'd never see the last of my possessions again, that the machine would eat everything and spit out only my winter-stained shoelaces. Standing behind the yellow line, staring at the officer with the shaved head and blue latex gloves on the other side of the metal detector, whose full attention was on a frumpy woman with mum jeans and eighties bangs, I flexed my toes with such force that I thought a foot cramp was about to cripple me, but it didn't. The officer waved me forward. As I stepped toward the metal detector, my heart threatened to beat through my chest and run away. I gazed at the handcuffs on his hip and could almost feel them tightening around my wrists. I gripped my right wrist and squeezed as I stepped through the monolithic archway—the officer stared at my chest the entire time.

Nothing beeped. The officer stepped aside, waving me through with his wand. I let go of my wrist and strolled past him; he turned his attention to the person behind me. When I noticed the officer with the clipboard looking at someone else, my bowels, which I hadn't even notice tightening into knots, relaxed, and I nearly shit myself. Stepping into my shoes and shoving my things into my bag, I hurried around the corner to the bathroom. I couldn't undo my pants fast enough, and liquified terror splashed into the bowl before I was fully seated, raining airport toilet water up onto my ass. Relief was immediate. Cleanup took a little longer.

At the sink, I splashed cold water on my face and looked at myself in the water-spotted mirror. Not even the purple and green bruise on the side of my face made the officers want to detain me. Maybe they thought it was a birthmark. A grotesque, fist-sized birthmark. More cold water on my face, it soothed the ache of the bruise that was suddenly throbbing and forcing my eyes to wince.

At the restroom entrance, I glanced back at security and knew I'd be long gone before they'd find out what I'd done and that they'd let me go. *If they found out at all.* Amy could keep a secret and would lie if she had to. Mercy might tell people, to brag and feel like a big shot, but he'd have to lie to make himself sound like the hero —and I wouldn't be in his version of what happened. I couldn't be. Not if he wanted a high five or whatever other praise he expected.

Security was more concerned with riffling through the bag of an Indian fellow and forcing him to remove his shoes before walking through the scanner again. They didn't care about someone already through.

Glad I wasn't that man, I smirked and turned toward my departure gate, glancing back over my shoulder just to make sure no one was following me.

As I sat next to the terminal staring at my one-way ticket and waiting for the clock with large red digits to catch up to my departure time, a black speck drew my eyes to the stained carpet beneath my feet. An ant scurried toward the soles of my shoes. Glancing around at all the other feet waiting at gate 53—some twitching like those of a kid with ADHD waiting outside of the principle's office, others tapping like metronomes for invisible instruments, but most still—I leaned over and put my finger down in front of the little guy. He hesitated, his feelers probing my skin for a second before he climbed on. I lifted him up in front of my face. When I focused on him, everything except for the tip of my finger and the ant blurred. His little feelers waved around on top of his bobbing head while his crab-claw mouth opened and closed. He kind of looked like a dog trying to smell me. I smiled and wanted to put him in my pocket and take him with me, to keep him safe from all of those feet stomping around the airport. We'd travel around the world together. I'd get him a little leash, maybe a dish with his name on it—something nobody would be able to read without a magnifying glass—some little booties for his feet in the winter. He'd be the perfect pet, and I'd never have to worry about picking up his microscopic poops.

Then he turned and looked back down at the carpet where another ant stood by my feet. *His girlfriend.* She looked up at him, feeling for him. He began to climb down my arm to get to her.

I thought of Lisa, felt the tears rush to my eyes, and lowered the little ant to the carpet. The two ants exchanged nods and then scurried away together through the gigantic maze that was their prison. I watched them until they disappeared into the mottled world of stained carpet and airport filth.

At least they have each other, I thought.

I began blinking slowly, my eyes heavy with exhaustion. I saw Lisa's face every time my eyes closed, tears threatening to burst through the images of her. If only she could have been there, sitting beside me with a matching ticket in one hand, her other hand holding mine, staring at me, her eyes poised like tidal waves about to break and drag me down into that endless blue.

I gasped for air, realizing I had stopped breathing for a moment. It was hard not to think about her. Hard not to feel suffocated by the thought of her. Hard not to wish for her to be with me and me with her. But that wasn't what she wanted. I never factored into her life. Not until the end of it.

Outside the huge wall of windows to my left, planes were taking off, landing, taxiing, and docking. I caught my breath watching their calculated movements. Beyond all the planes and waving batons and luggage trains, past the runways and the fences and the distant trees was the moon. It hung just above the horizon, the blood red colour from last night had drain from it. It still looked full though and grew more pronounced as the sun set the earth on fire with its kiss somewhere on the opposite side of the airport.

The sun was setting behind the airport but rising in front of another, and I was going to chase it and greet it on the other side.

Chapter 2

Scanning the stupid smiley face mouse pads, the excessive surround sound speakers, and the overpriced power bars that protect against every kind of power surge imaginable—all of which the guy would probably never experience in his lifetime—I thought about the extra fifteen dollar commission I was about to make off the 'surge protector' in my hands and broke into my spiel about warranty.

"Now, the only thing left to decide is which Merchandise Protection Strategy you wanna go with today," I said, nodding and grinning like an idiot, my free hand taking out the brochure from my back pocket and flipping it open.

I snuck in a line about how limited the manufacture's warranty is at the first computer we looked at, like I was taught. Slipped in how he'd have to send away the computer when he asked about the hard drive, and I told him it could crash. Told him that five percent of all computers are lemons, a statistic printed in a scary looking font on my Merchandise Protection Strategy Sheet that we now looked at together.

"How much is the warranty?" the guy asked with a sigh, clearly reaching his accessory breaking point.

Always the first question. I had the prices memorized but I said, "Let's see," tracing my finger from *Computer* to *Two Years*. "For two years it'll be one hundred and twenty-five."

He exhaled as if trying to blow out candles on his fortieth birthday cake on a day, which was also, the anniversary of his wife leaving him, taking all his money, and shacking up with his best friend. I could smell his lunch—a combination of hotdog, ketchup, and the kind of halitosis that smells like shit with a hint of sulphur. Resisting the urge to wave the stench away from my face, I leaned away slightly, pretended he hadn't just farted out of his mouth, and I said, "Three years is one seventy-five and four years is two seventy-five."

I dropped the warranty price sheet, which I had laminated myself with packing tape and a utility knife, to my side.

"I know it's expensive but it's worth it."

He looked on the verge of saying no, so I said, "A guy just came in last week and got a brand new computer for free because his motherboard was fried. And he bought his computer three and a half years ago, so the computer he got was way better than his old one. If he hadn't bought the four-year warranty, I would've had to sell him that computer instead of just giving it to him."

I liked telling that story because it really happened and wasn't just some made up crap handed down from Dan Dan the manager man. I got to help a guy pick out a computer that was of equal value to one he had bought almost four years prior. At the till he told me he wanted the four-year warranty on the new one; I didn't even have to ask him or explain it or sell him on it. I just rang it in, carried the new computer out to his truck, and made a cool hundred bucks in ten minutes. It was the perfect sale. The commission on most computers is only around thirty bucks. As I told the story, I wished I could give away computers and only sell the commission-sweet warranty all the time.

"Why is it so expensive for four years?" he asked, right on cue.

"Good question," I said. "It's because something is more likely to go wrong the older the computer gets." I gave it a moment to sink in and watched him rub the back of his neck. "I usually recommend three years. It's the most bang for your buck, and you're covered for *three years*."

"All right," he said, sighing again, his breath turning even more sour. "I'll go with the three year."

I turned my back to him and rang it all in. There is always this weird tension after I talk someone into buying warranty; it manifests itself as an indigestible brick sitting in my stomach. Customers feel forced into buying something they don't really want, and I feel like a fraud because I've sold them this intangible thing that they will probably never use. I've stolen their money, we both know it, but they aren't going to accuse me, and I'm not going to confess, and all we want is to get away from each other.

While double checking that I'd scanned every barcode, Charlie—a veteran computer salesman in his mid twenties and the guy who had trained me when I was hired three years ago—walked up and leaned into me. He started sniffing as if he had just finished snorting some coke in a bathroom stall. The weight of him forced me to the side and my legs to bear down. Staring at the computer screen he whispered, "That smells pretty fucking good," while nudging me with his shoulder a couple of times.

"That's a great machine you have there," Charlie said, leaning back and addressing my customer.

"It should do the trick."

"It's the same one my parents have. They love it."

Charlie turned back to me. "Can you come see me when you're done?"

"Sure."

"Enjoy the computer," Charlie said, smiling and walking away.

I handed over the receipt and walked with him to his car, pushing a cart full of stuff. He popped the trunk, revealing a spare tire, empty water bottles, fast-food napkins, and several plastic bags full of junk. He looked at me; I turned and looked back at the store as if I hadn't just seen what a fucking slob he was, pretending not to be thinking about his hoarder's apartment packed ceiling high with boxes of junk, a lifetime of old phonebooks and mail, the body of a forgotten ferret rotting and squished beneath a collapsed pile of newspapers. I imagined the narrow path that let him move from the kitchen to the living room to bed, his bathroom completely barricaded with shit and forcing him to use old pots as toilets.

It'd be like living in his mouth, I thought, wanting to puke.

He pulled a chunk of carpet over the tire and garbage, and I lifted his purchases inside.

"Do you live nearby?"

"Just over the hill."

He shut the trunk gently, careful not to crush anything. I wanted to run back inside. The smile on my face was making my cheeks hurt.

"Well," I said, expecting him to change his mind and return everything. "Enjoy your new computer. If you have any questions don't hesitate to call."

I walked back inside—*please hesitate*—and checked out the one hundred seventy-eight dollar commission I'd just made.

"How's that sale smell?" Kurt, the nasal-voiced assistant manager, said leaning over my shoulder. He sniffed a couple times while checking out my numbers. He reeked of old spice and some sort of gel that kept his short black hair glued tightly to his head. "Why didn't you get full stink?" he said, almost squealing.

'Full stink' is what everyone in the store calls the maximum warranty on a product and the longer the warranty the higher the commission. Everyone walks around sniffing while you're with a customer. After a sale they ask, 'Did you get full stink?' or after their own sales say, 'I just sold a fifty inch with full stink' or 'Half stink and batteries.' Batteries are accessories, everything not included.

"I got three years," I said.

Kurt shook his head. "Only three years on this one. And you had a couple go out without stink at all last week." His tone was that of a disappointed principle. "At least you got some nice batteries attached."

He lifted up his clipboard and flipped through a few pages, obviously checking out my sales.

"Your numbers are slipping though."

He looked up at me like a disapproving father who steals from my piggy bank and then complains about not getting enough money.

"You gotta get your numbers up."

I wanted to bite his nose off and spit it back at his bloodied face.

"Why do you still print that stuff off? We work in an electronics store. Get a tablet at least."

Kurt dropped his clipboard to his side and raised his eyebrows. "If I had a tablet, I'd still be seeing your less-than-stellar numbers. Are you going to get them up?"

"I'll try."

"You better do more than try. Don't you remember what Dan said at the meeting on Sunday?"

I was trying to forget everything Dan had ever said and every meeting that I was forced to attend on my days off.

***

"Before we get started today," Dan said, "I just wanna ask everyone one question."

Smiles and giggles rippled through the crowd of employees like The Wave around a packed stadium. Everyone knew what question was coming because Dan yelled the same question at every morning meeting. Everyone stood up in anticipation. The beginning of the meetings were like my elementary school choir practices. Mrs. Shoemaker would make us all stand before she conducted us. I only lipped the words during choir practice just like I only lipped the response after Dan would yell, "GOOD MORNING."

"GOOD MORNING," everyone except me yelled back.

"HOW IS EVERYONE DOING THIS MORNING?" Dan asked while his face turned red and the pulsing vein in his forehead looked like it was going to burst and spray on the fans in the front row.

"GREAT," the choir sang.

"AND WHAT ARE WE GOING TO DO THIS MORNING?" he yelled this question even louder, his face turning from blood red to greedy purple.

"MAKE MONEY," the choir sang, their faces only a slightly lighter shade than Dan's.

"AND HOW ARE WE GOING TO MAKE MONEY?"

"BY SELLING."

"All right. Take a seat," Dan said, breathing heavy, allowing his face to return to a normal colour. He should have said take a knee because he was more like a coach than a boss.

I continued to think about Mrs. Shoemaker; part of me felt as if I were back in her class. She was my grade four homeroom teacher and a lot nicer than Dan. She read to us, lit incense and got us to meditate—which mostly consisted of deep breaths and trying not to think of anything—she also gave us treats when we were good. All Dan ever gave me was a headache.

Mrs. Shoemaker's graciousness didn't stop the class from calling her Mrs. Poobaker when she wasn't listening or from writing nasty things about her in our textbooks when she was within earshot or when there was a substitute teacher or when boredom seemed to make the pencil write on its own. When I sat back down to listen to Dan finally speak without yelling, I thought about the day Mrs. Shoemaker realized the class, her class, had vandalized every textbook. The books were communal, so, unless she tried to match our handwriting, there was no way of knowing who'd written what. So instead of getting us to confess, she forced us to read what was written in our books aloud. We had to read to the entire class while Mrs. Shoemaker patrolled the classroom, her clicking high heels a constant reminder that she was listening.

Some students wrote declarations of undying love like *Sarah plus Ryan forever* or built upon what others had written like *Ryan's cute* or *Ryan has a big forehead.* Mostly, there were insults. Funny at first, until I heard my own name. It was something silly about this zit I'd had in the middle of my forehead a few months earlier. *Felix is a unicorn* or something like that. All of our heads drooped lower and lower as we read and read and read. *I hate Stephanie. Jason smells like shit.* Mrs. Shoemaker's heels, as she stomped around the classroom, clicked against the floor louder and louder with each reading, but the clicking stopped after I read.

"Go ahead Felix," she said, "read it to the class."

I didn't want to but everyone was looking at me and waiting. The silence felt like a spotlight shining on me. I hadn't written it so, convincing myself it was no big deal, I read it as fast as I could. "Mrs. Poobaker eats her own cookies."

I could feel Mrs. Shoemaker's eyes burning into the top of my head as I stared down at my book, at the ugly words and worse printing. It was the only thing written there, so I waited for her to ask the next student to read. But she said, "Please read that again, Felix. A little slower this time."

I read it again and, even though I didn't write it, I felt guilty.

"Is that all?" she asked. I nodded. "Daniel?" She cleared her throat. "What's in your book?"

"Mrs. Poobaker makes shitty cookies."

A few kids snickered. Daniel allowed a smirk to flash across his face. Mrs. Shoemaker didn't make a sound, so we all slowly raised our heads. She tottered to her reading chair—her heels clicking sporadically—and sat down. At first it sounded like she was laughing, her face in her hands, muffling her spasmodic chuckles. When she sniffed, we all knew she was crying and felt damp with her tears. Then she sobbed, loud and forceful tears that were completely unrestrained. We all glanced at each other wondering what to do. Nobody moved. As I sat there listening to my fourth grade teacher cry, I wished I had thought to erase instead of read. At that moment, as if Mrs. Shoemaker read my mind, she stood up, wiped her eyes, and told us all to take out our erasers—*sniff sniff*—and begin the purge. Yet no matter how hard I pushed with that eraser, the words were still visible—etched into the inside of the book's cover forever.

While staring at the floor and thinking about those etched words, an ant marched around on the cheap hospital tiles of the store floor. His jerky movements made him look as if he were hitting walls while trying to weave through a maze.

"Before we get started," Dan said, "I just want to give you the three stars for last week. Nigel, stand up .... Nigel made seven hundred and eighty dollars last week with eighty-five percent warranty."

Everyone clapped, but the noise and Dan's voice suddenly disappeared as I watched the ant. It was just me and him. A smile began to creep across my face like a mouse peeking out of its hiding place while a cat lurks nearby. Just before some teeth began to show under my cracking lips and tender thoughts of where the ant came from occupied my mind, a black leather boot stepped and smeared until the ant was only a skid mark on the cold floor. I almost felt him squish into oblivion, and my grimace brought me back to the noise of the meeting and the congratulatory jerk-off session that was underway. The boot belonged to the woman beside me, and she didn't even notice what she had done. She clapped like a maniac, hooted, and continued to chew her gum like an ape chewing gum for the very first time.

"And our number one star is Jamal with fifteen hundred dollars and one hundred percent warranty." Dan threw his clipboard under his arm and clapped with such force that his claps sounded like balloons popping. "Give it up for Jamal. Nice work, buddy."

As the clapping roared on, all I could think of was squashing the woman under my heel or stabbing her with the pen I was supposed to be writing notes with. Everyone had pens and was expected to write notes. I never made notes. My pen, as always, rested lifelessly in my hand, but finally I thought of a reason to bring it to life.

While I gripped the pen, I couldn't help thinking about what I should do if I did stab her; whether I should break the submerged end of the pen off inside her like a good old prison shanking or whether a series of Hitchcockesque stabbings would feel better.

Her leg would be the first to get it because the damn thing wouldn't stop shaking. She was like a dog being scratched behind the ear except no one was gratifying her faithful itch. She was the most awful person I had ever observed and had the misfortune to sit beside. When she pulled out Kleenex, she didn't aim for a discreet *I hope nobody notices* blow. She just blew while alternating which nostril she pressed shut and then opened the Kleenex to looked at her mucus. Then when she'd finished blowing, she held her crumpled, snot rag between her index finger and thumb as if it were a disgusting piece of garbage she had just found. Her nose was making sweet love to the Kleenex a split second earlier and ejaculating all over it, but, after she'd finished, she acted like the Kleenex was a strange baby's poopy diaper. So she dropped it on the floor— leaving her mucus-covered waste for someone else to clean up—and wiped her hands clean on the bottom of her chair.

Although I was getting closer and closer to stabbing her, I couldn't stop watching her. It was like watching the surgery channel; it's a gross, anxiety-inducing experience, but for some reason it's mesmerizing.

Trying to forget about her and to avoid looking at the black smear that used to be an inquisitive ant, I turned to Dan..

"Now, I realize that everybody here has lives outside of this building, but once you step through those doors," he gestured behind himself toward the front doors, "you should be ready for the task at hand and leave your lives outside where they belong."

Crack, crack, crack!

Just when I had tuned her out, she began to crack every bone in her left hand and then the mirroring bones in her right, the popping echoed inside my head. I wanted to stab her more than ever just then and put her out of my misery. The name of the store we both worked for, SUPER COMPUTERS, which was emblazoned on the pen, would lacerate her heart and create a shocked silence in the room ... or would it? I guess it wouldn't have mattered anyway if I killed her because apparently her life, along with everyone else's, was outside the building's entrance waiting for her— she was already dead.

I wanted to make a break for it, to run out and straight arm Dan like a running back heading for the end zone. My end zone was a coffee shop where Mercy wanted to meet. I almost laughed out loud at the realization that I wanted to rush to see Mercy to escape the meeting, to trade one irritating person for another. Even if I had left right then, he'd have been his usual tardy self. Mercy doesn't mind making people wait. In his world, time is thirty minutes slower than real time. When he finally shows up, he dismisses his tardiness

21

and bites his nails; nail clippers don't exist in his world. As if the horrible clicking and snapping of his nails between his teeth isn't rude enough, he spits the chewed up bits out. It doesn't matter where he is either; inside or out, his bedroom or my bedroom, the kitchen or the living room, a restaurant or a movie theatre, wherever he is when he needs to spit out his gnawed nails, he does it. He just turns his head to the side and spits, the way you'd spit when trying to remove a small hair from the tip of your tongue.

Just then, the woman started nibbling her nails. At least with Mercy I can tell him to stop. When Mercy is gnawing on his fingers, I can just say, 'Stop it! Stop biting your goddamn nails! It's disgusting.'

I wanted to turn to her and say, *Stop shaking or I'll rip off your leg and beat you to death with it.* What I really wanted to do was resort to some of Mercy's teenaged antics: turn to her and ask, *Who married Mary the cow?* And when she responded by saying, *What?* I'd punch her in the leg as hard as I could while yelling, *Charlie Horse!* Or maybe I should have held her down and farted on her head; Mercy really loved that one. Childish brotherly love probably wouldn't have gone over well with all my coworkers. Some may have laughed, but I would have been fired for sure and most likely charged. *Is farting on somebody's head considered assault?*

I'd never do that to anyone though because I could probably use therapy for all the fartboarding I endured as a kid. I'm thankful that my sister and I shared in the stench tortures otherwise I might have gotten Prolonged Flatulence Exposure Syndrome (PFES) resulting in brain damage, which would have been really embarrassing for my parents to explain to people.

Growing up, Amy's biggest peeve with Mercy was the way he would scratch the white gunk off of his teeth and then look at it before eating it.

"You know if you brushed your teeth occasionally, you wouldn't have that film on your teeth and I wouldn't have to get grossed out by your disgusting scratching," Amy would say.

I have to admit that I used to scratch my teeth too sometimes, but I was always alone when I did it, and I never did it at the dinner table like Mercy. To Amy's point though, I never brushed my teeth growing up so a good brushing would've cleaned that stuff for sure. Young boys have poorer hygiene than young girls but eventually boys catch up or at least some of them do.

If Amy were at that meeting with me she would have, without any hesitation, just asked the woman to stop shaking and moving around so much. Not me. That would be too easy. I just sat there and stewed, thinking that somehow the woman was going to read my mind and stop fidgeting. Why couldn't I have just asked her politely to stop? Or moved farther away from her?

"So if you make money," Dan said, "then the company makes money, and everyone's happy. You look good, your managers look good, and I look good."

That was really all that mattered to him.

"If everyone does their share, the *team* looks good and there is no I in *team*, but everyone needs to take care of themselves and make sure that they're doing the best job possible, to make themselves the most money possible."

What? So there is no 'I in Team' but I'm only supposed to think about myself. I wished an invisible hand would strangle Dan. All the managers cared about was money, which was why everyone was sitting there an hour before their scheduled start time and not getting paid for it; it was also why I was sitting there on my day off and not getting paid.

"So whoever wants to make money, whoever wants to enjoy a fat paycheck, whoever wants to go home and be happy after a day's work, needs to sell. Sell warranty.

Sell accessories. Sell yourselves. Now I'm gonna open up the doors in a coupla minutes, so make sure your departments are good to go and ready for customers. Okay guys? Let's sell and make some money."

Then everyone clapped as usual. Dan's shoulders heaved while he clapped way too enthusiastically. I put my hands in my pockets when the clapping started.

Everyone moved toward their departments.

"Remember to sell warranty. That's where the big money is, and we have to keep our numbers up because we're in third place for the top store in all of Canada. And remember the party we get if we're number one. Sell. Sell. Sell."

That was it. No Thanks for coming in on your day off. Keep up the good work. I should have quit, right then.

Everyone got to work, and the annoying woman kicked my chair as she walked away.

***

Kurt stared at me waiting for an answer? "Do you remember what Dan said on Sunday," Kurt asked again.

I shut off my commission screen and faced him. "Yeah, I remember."

"Well, one of the last things he said was, sell warranty," he said, making bunny ears with both hands, adding quotation marks to his words with his fingers.

"What does that mean?" I asked, knowing exactly what the gesture meant.

"What?"

I mimicked the quoting gesture.

"It means that I'm quoting Dan."

"Do you always finger paint punctuation in the air around your words?" I said, drawing a question mark in the air.

"You better watch yourself."

"Shouldn't you put an exclamation point after that?" I drew a question mark again. "Otherwise I won't know how to take it." I poked the air to add a period.

Kurt put his clipboard under his arm and scrunched up his forehead.

"And, for the record, I did sell warranty. I got three years."

"It's not as good as four. Be more like Jamal. Get full stink every time. Okay?" He strolled away and then turned to point at me with his eyebrows raised before turning back around.

If I would have had a snowball, I would have hit Kurt in the back of the head with it as he walked toward the office. He was a little weasel, paid to get on everyone's case. He deserved a snowball to the head. I had never wished for spring to turn into winter until that moment, but Kurt needed to get pelted to death with snowballs.

While walking to the printer section, I glanced at my watch. I had three hours left. *God, kill me now.* Just then, my phone vibrated against my thigh. It was Mercy, calling a few days early, and I hadn't talked to him since we met up last Sunday after my work meeting.

I hadn't really wanted to see him that Sunday because he said he had a deal for me, which I knew probably meant he could get a two for one gym membership and wanted to split it with me regardless of the fact that I don't go to the gym anymore. I stopped going a while ago. I used to run for a bit but stopped that too. Mercy didn't care about that or even realize it. He used to play every sport—at least every sport that encouraged hurting the opposing team and cultivated a pugilistic atmosphere. Hockey was his blood sport of choice. Mercy often had to miss the end of the season of whatever sport he was biding his time with until hockey started up again. He'd drop his lacrosse racket or football cleats and quit as easily as he'd drop his hockey gloves for a fight. Maybe that was why Mercy loved playing hockey so much, he could beat someone up and be back the next game. I used to watch him play sometimes. Because Mercy fought so much, he could drop his gloves and have his helmet off before his opponent and way before the boxing bell rang—*ding*. He was like Billy the Kid, nobody could get the drop on him. Once, a guy he wanted to fight dropped his gloves but didn't take off his helmet. It was the only fight I'd ever seen Mercy lose. He punched the guy's visor and broke his hand. Then while trying to unclip the guy's helmet, his nose was broken after three quick punches—*bap, bap, CRACK*. The refs broke it up about the time a pint of blood congealed on the ice. Mercy, with red streaming down his face, kept calling his unscathed opponent a pussy as he skated off the ice.

To Mercy, playing sports meant having to work out during downtime. Muscle magazines of every month and publication were always littered throughout my parents' house as his source of muscle-building inspiration and instruction. At one point, I think he strived to look just like the guys in the magazines. It might have been just another distraction to help kill

28

time until hockey started up again, but he started buying baby oil and greasing himself up and flexing in front of a mirror; he may have even entered an amateur flexing competition once, but I can't really remember.

On Sunday, Mercy said nothing of a gym membership. He walked into the café, gave me the patented Mercy nod and smirk that always put a single word in my mind as if through telepathy—*sup*—and then he went straight to the bar for a beer, no glass. The barista was a midnight-haired, azure-eyed beauty who made me lose my words when I tried to order my clover coffee. When she placed a bottle in front of Mercy, he gave her a bill and said, "It's all you," while leaning toward her and winking the way he leans forward and winks at every woman. The barista took the money and left the bait. She instantly became a goddess to me; my lust for her abated by pangs of respect, admiration, and envy.

With beer in hand, Mercy walked over to me, the arms of his sunglasses pinching his neck, letting his Oakley sunglasses hang down onto his chest, his backwards baseball hat a little too high off his head, his flip flops smack smack smacking the soles of his feet with every step—he looked like a douche.

"Hey buddy!" he said while pulling out the empty chair beside me and sitting down.

"How's it going?" I said.

"Ah, you know." He took a sip of beer and looked around the café. "Do you like this place?"

"It's pretty cool. Amy told me about this place too. She lives right around here."

"Oh, yeah. Well, I knew you'd like it." He looked back at the barista. "I like the scenery."

Then he downed his beer. Mercy could open his throat and finish an entire beer in seconds. It was a talent he'd always had and always broke out at parties. He waved the empty bottle at the barista.

"Ahh, that's better."

The goddess came over to our table carrying a fresh beer.

"Thanks," Mercy said when she put the beer on the table in front of him.

She was wearing a tight, sleeveless shirt, her flat belly and pierced naval peeking out from beneath it. She said, "Three seventy-five," but I heard, *Go fuck yourself.*

Mercy held out a five. "Keep the change," he said, passing her the empty by sticking his middle finger in it and almost flicking it in her direction.

She smirked and turned. Mercy and I watched her walk away, almost hypnotized by her sway and bounce in tight jeans.

"Mmm," Mercy groaned. "I forgot to ask her to sit on my face."

"She'd probably say no," I said, still watching her.

"Did you see that ass?" he turned to me. "Oh, look at you."

I turned to him. "What?"

"You're still seeing it even though she's behind the bar. You'll probably see it tonight too when you're spitting on your cock because you forgot to buy lube on the way home." He leaned back, smug.

My mouth was open but I said nothing. He was right, I didn't have lube and, at that moment, I probably wanted her more than I had ever wanted anyone, but I didn't want Mercy to know that. I didn't want him to think we were the same. We weren't the same. Not even close. I tried to push the sexual thoughts out of my mind.

"Just use olive oil," he said, glancing back at the bar. "Yeah, she's nice."

"Nice?" Mercy leaned forward. "Nice? That, my friend, is a thing of beauty. God, I wanna eat it."

Mercy twisted off the bottle cap—*tsst*—and took a drink, making a satisfied groan as if he had just crawled through the desert and eaten only sand for two days; it reminded me of an awful beer commercial.

Glancing around to see if any of the other patrons were perturbed with the spectacle, I sighed and said, "How's the beer?" as Mercy wiped his mouth with the back of his beer-holding hand.

"It's the best thing for a hangover." He leaned forward. "Oh, you should have been there last night, buddy. It was great. Nothin' but kegs and girls." He grinned at me through glazed bloodshot eyes.

"Did you ask me here to tell me about last night's sex? Because I'm really not interested in hearing more stories about anal intruders right now." I took a sip of my coffee, strong thick and wonderful.

"I didn't."

"Good."

"Now that you mention it, there was this Nikki girl there last night that came up to me and told me to give her a call when I cut my hair," he said, smiling.

"That's great, Murse."

Mercy always told me stories that seemed to come out of smut magazines. At first, I thought they were exciting tales of adventure and sex. A few I really got into. I even used to fantasize about being in some of the same situations he told me about. He had a few stories about threesomes and one-night stands that I still think about sometimes. I didn't really want to hear it anymore though. Listening to the play-by-play commentary from pickup line to him sneaking out of the girl's house felt like reading a book I already knew the ending to. He recounted a new escapade every time I saw him. I'd say I didn't want to hear it, but he never seemed to hear me, and I couldn't just tell him I didn't give a shit because he *loved* telling me about them.

"It's more than great. I've wanted her forever."

"Why? She doesn't strike you as the shallow type?"

"I don't care what type she is. She's hot." He took a sip.

To tell Mercy that he should look for a relationship with more substance would be like telling a penis to not get erect when it's hungry.

"So did you sleep with her?"

He lifted his backwards hat to reveal his matted rat's nest beneath. "I gotta get a haircut first." He readjusted his hat. "She didn't even touch my sausage … well, she may have brushed up against it by accident, but she didn't stroke it or anything."

"So when's your hair appointment?"

"I haven't made one yet." He leaned back and took a swig of beer. "I'm lettin' her sweat." Another swig.

"So, you said you had a deal for me," I said, wanting to get out of there fast. "What is it?"

"Oh, yeah. If you let me borrow your car next week, I'll forget about that fifty bucks you owe me." He tilted his bottle toward me and winked as if he were a cowboy offering not to kill me if I gave him my horse.

"What fifty bucks?"

"The fifty bucks from the hockey ticket you never used."

"What hockey ticket?"

"Last month. I had to get Kyle to go with me."

"I had to work. You bought the ticket and then asked me."

"You said you wanted to see a game."

"Yeah. Sometime. When we can both go."

"Whatever, I'm offering you a way out of it."

"Out of what?"

"Owing me the fifty."

"Fine then, you owe me a hundred bucks to pay for half of my Alfred Hitchcock box set you borrowed and still haven't given back."

"That's totally different."

"Is it? Take fifty off what I owe you for the ticket and then you only owe me fifty."

Mercy leaned forward and raised his voice a little. "Fine. Then I'll take the fifty bucks you owe me from the house-boating trip last summer."

"What house-boating trip?"

"Remember? You said you'd come and then didn't."

"I never said I'd go. And, again, I never even went so how can I owe you for that?" I would have spit coffee in his face if it wasn't so delicious.

"I don't know why you're being like this," he said, adjusting his hat a bit. "I'm trying to do you a favour."

"Being like what? Reasonable? You know, if you want to borrow my car, all you have to do is ask."

"Fine." He took a swig and ran his tongue over his teeth. "Can I borrow your car?" He said, his eyes turned up to the ceiling.

"What for?"

"God. What does it matter? I just need it, okay."

"What's wrong with your car?"

"I don't know." He sat back and crossed his arms. "It won't start. Probably the alternator. Can I borrow it or not?"

"Sure." I didn't feel like arguing with him anymore. "When do you need it?"

He stopped pouting a little. "Next Monday."

"That's fine. I have that Monday off anyway."

He downed his beer and stood up. "Cool. I'll probably come by in the morning to pick it up." He turned to leave and said, "See ya later, buddy," over his shoulder.

***

I wandered—holding my phone until it stopped vibrating, staring at Mercy's name and phone number the entire time—into the printer section where Victoria and Charlie stood talking. Then I lifted my gaze to my coworkers.

"I'm gonna win it," Charlie said, chewing his gum like a child, his mouth open, his juicy flavoured lips smacking together with every chomp. Charlie's gum chewing made his pronounced underbite—like that of an old, stinky dog that should have been put down years ago—his facial focal point. Like a facial birthmark or lady moustache, Charlie's flapping and protruding jaw made it impossible to look anywhere else.

"You have to have the most computers sales nationwide," Victoria said, her shiny black hair looked sticky and sweet like liquorice, which might have explained why a clump of hair was always in her mouth. The bob hairstyle probably didn't help since a flick of her head could toss hair right in there. She curled a finger around the moist clump of hair and fished it out of her mouth. "It's impossible."

"I'm in third right now," Charlie said, "I just have to outsell everybody for three months."

"Good luck with that."

"Felix."

I heard Charlie say my name but let my eyes fall down to the words MISSED CALL displayed on my phone.

"Are you gunning for the ten grand?"

"What ten grand?" I said, putting my phone in my pocket and looking him straight in the underbite.

"It's a prize for selling a ridiculous amount of computers," Victoria said.

"Probably not." My head suddenly felt like it was being squeezed in a vice, one of my eyes threatening to pop out of its socket. The florescent lights humming high above us seemed brighter than the sun; I had to squint a little to bare the glare but not so much that Victoria and Charlie noticed.

"I know. It's impossible."

"It's not impossible," Charlie said. "I can win. And, if I do, I'll finally quit."

"Didn't you try to quit already?"

"Yeah but when Dan told me I was a contender for the ten large, I decided to stay. It's only three more months."

"After you win, let's all quit," Victoria said.

I wanted to quit right then. To take off my pukey blue collared shirt, throw it in Kurt's face, and walk out. I didn't need to say the words to Dan, never seeing him again would be enough satisfaction. It was either quit or get a head transplant, the only two solutions I could think of until I remembered that I had migraine drugs in the secret coin pocket of my pants.

"Why are you squinting?"

"Am I?" I looked to Victoria who nodded. "The lights. They're bright aren't they?"

"No brighter than usual," Victoria said.

"You kinda look like Clint Eastwood right now, Squinty," Charlie said.

"Hey, that reminds me, have you seen that new movie with Christian Bale?"

"Which one?"

Movies. Why is it always movies? People always end up talking about movies at one point in the conversation. Usually if there is a pause. Talking about movies keeps a conversation on failing life support. The worst is when somebody asks, *Have you seen any good movies lately?* Doesn't anyone have anything more interesting to say? Just let the conversation die. Pull the fucking plug already.

"I watched it last night; it was awesome."

"Yeah, it's great, hey."

The worst is when people get so excited about nothing. It's just a movie.

"I loved it. Felix, have you seen it?"

I shook my head wondering how a person could love a movie. Then movie talk went into overdrive. My head was in a trash compactor and both my eyes were going to pop out and swing down from coils of veins, arteries, and nerves, dangling by my mouth.

—Have you seen this?

—Yeah, have you seen that?

—She's my favourite.

—He's mine.

—I want to see the new this.

—Well, have you seen the new that?

—There's a new that?

—Yeah, I saw it yesterday.

—I've got to see it!

I wondered what eyes tasted like. If I'd feel relief if my head exploded. How long I had to stand there pretending not to hate both Victoria and Charlie. I stuck my finger into that tight coin pocket and fingered the smooth gel cap.

Who uses coins anymore? And why are pants still manufactured with a coin pocket?

I glanced around at all the printers, inkjet and laser, all-in-ones with fax machines, the toner, the cables. *And who the fuck buys printers these days? What's the point? Let it go. Jesus. And fax machines. Really? You need a printer with a fax? Bullshit. Dive into the twenty-first century, the water's warm and digital. Use PDFs.* The only printers that should be sold are 3D ones. Maybe I could use one of them to print me out a new, non-migraine prone head.

"I'll be back," I said, interrupting them and not caring what part of their movie conversation I had just disrupted.

"Hey," Charlie said, "where are you going?"

"To pee."

Walking toward the bathroom, the bright lights above me felt like icepicks stabbing my retinas. I took the little gel pill out of my pocket; it had the number 400 on it and a seam all the way around its oval centre. I placed it on my tongue and swallowed hard. The pill got stuck somewhere in my throat so, once at the washroom, I chugged water from the stainless-steel fountain between the ladies' and the men's. As the pill slid down, I felt instantly better even though I knew the drug wouldn't kick in for a while.

Inside the washroom, Raj stood at one of the sinks washing his hands.

"Hey," he said.

He had perfect skin and sported a couple days worth of dark beard growth, which was unusual for Mr. Cleanshaven. Until that moment I thought his daily shaving habits were a part of his religious rituals.

I nodded and stood in front of the other sink. Holding my hand under the motion-sensor faucet, I let the water run over the back of my hand until it was glacier cold. Then I cupped and doused my face over and over and over, the *whoosh* of the water halted when I lifted my hands to my face and sputtered on again when my hands returned underneath the spout. Rubbing an icy hand on the back of my neck, I breathed deeply, concentrating on not throwing up.

"You okay?"

"Yeah," I said. "You?"

"What do you mean?"

I rubbed my chin and gave a slight flick of my head toward him.

"Oh." He glanced at himself in the mirror, ran a palm down the side of his face. "Right."

His face drooped almost imperceptibly. As he lowered his hand, his silver wristwatch caught my eye. At first I wanted to put wristwatch wearer into the some category as printer and fax machine buyers, but then I began longing to have his watch on my wrist. It looked comforting, grounding, sure of itself.

"Me and Ansley broke up."

"Oh."

Ansley was the girl Raj hadn't shut up about for the last three months. He talked to everyone about her. Showed off pictures, discussed date plans, conversed about gift ideas—month, two-month, three-month anniversary presents. So naturally I thought, *Thank God, now you won't be talking about her every time your mouth is open.* But Raj was a decent guy, and my headache was ebbing, and he had a fantastic watch, so I turned to face him.

"I thought everything was good with you two."

"It was. Except for the last month."

"What happened?"

"I told you how I'm a virgin right?"

Oh yeah, he's a virgin, with the word practically tattooed to his forehead in the bolded letters of an awful font that he chose. I could almost see the word on his forehead, the Times New Roman characters practically yelling it at me—it certainly wasn't tattooed in Chinese characters; nobody had to ask, 'What does your tattoo say?' 'It says *One who has not experienced intercourse* in Chinese.' Raj had a palpable aura of naiveté and longing, the kind that comes when a person arbitrarily denies himself something like alcohol or caffeine or reason and then touts the abstention as virtuous while also practically nailing himself to a cross for all to see.

"Right," I said, trying not to give too much attention to his attention seeking.

"I'm a Christian."

Of course you are, I thought.

"Ansley's a Christian too just she sees nothing wrong with having sex before marriage."

Makes sense. "So she's not a virgin?"

"No."

"And you've never?"

"No."

"Not even just the tip?"

"No, nothing."

"Because of God?"

"And other reasons, yes."

"Don't you think God likes watching people have sex?"

"The married ones, yes."

"And he doesn't just turn a blind eye to all the unmarried sex going on?"

"According to Ansley he does."

"Is this why you broke up?"

"I can be intimate without sex. And I'm fine with that."

Because you don't know what you're missing, I wanted to say. *It's easy to deny yourself something you've never experienced.*

"But it wasn't enough for her, and we you know, just stopped clicking."

I don't fucking care. Just finish your story and get out so my head can throb in peace.

"I'm okay. Everything changed about a month ago, so I've had a month to get used to the idea that we might break up."

He crossed his arms and there was that watch again, on display and winking at me.

"I'll be okay," he said.

It had roman numerals, simple black characters that made the watch even more precious.

"I'll find someone whose values align with my own."

The inspirational, self-help book quotes only made me care more about the watch. The shiny silver a perfect compliment to the white watch face. The strap tightly interwoven threads of white nylon that matched the face. The white strap was a little much but it worked. I might have traded it in for a navy one with a single white stripe down the middle.

"That's probably for the best," I said, my headache making it impossible to filter the disinterest out of my voice.

"I think I might have found her," he said, his voice growing excited.

He pulled out his phone, swiped and flicked the display with a finger, and stepped closer to me. When he held out the phone, it displayed a picture of a girl that was clearly an online profile photo that he'd saved. The girl looked pouty and dough-eyed with an innocent expression that was also insidiously sexual —'I'll call you daddy,' she seemed to be whispering, 'but I don't know what that means.'

"Her name's Jessica," he turned the phone around to look at the picture. "We're going to meet up when she gets back from her parents' cabin."

I nodded.

Raj put his phone away, ran a hand through his hair while looking in the mirror, smiled at his reflection, a smile that made his eyes water, that made me pity him and regret my hostility toward him, a smile that was one of the saddest I've ever seen—an expression of pain loneliness and confusion, bordering on despair.

"Thanks," he said, patting me on the shoulder before leaving the washroom.

His gratitude put my heartbeat right in my forehead. I hadn't done anything. He could've had the same conversation with the mirror and had the same results. The mirror wouldn't have hated every second of the monologue either, wouldn't have hated him for being his own worst enemy.

I lingered at the sink, waiting for the pounding to subside, squeezing my eyes shut.

Why didn't you just have sex with her you poor God-fearing fuck?

As I stood hunched over the sink, the palm of my hand pressed against the damp sink of the public washroom, my arm straight and propping me up, I tried to rub the pain out of my head by massaging my neck with my free hand. Then I heard the door to one of the bathroom stalls creak open, the sound like ice water being injected into my right ear. I didn't want to open my eyes for fear of killing the person who caused the horrid sound, but when I didn't hear any footsteps or the other faucet spurt on or the bathroom door open and shut behind a germ-ridden man about to wipe fecal matter onto everything he touched, I winked my left eye open and then my right. Gazing straight ahead into the mirror, the reflection of a little boy stared back at me; he was maybe seven years old, standing at the sink, waving his hands around beneath the faucet, trying desperately to trigger the motion-sensor that wouldn't cooperate with him. I watched him for a moment, his little mouth hanging open in concentration, a blond cowlick sticking up on the top of his head—a stubborn golden lock that had probably popped up at some point throughout the day regardless of how forcefully it had been combed down in the morning by his mother. He wore a plaid button-up with sleeves rolled to the elbows; the shirt was tucked into jeans also rolled up and revealing blindingly bright pink socks. I wanted to think he dressed himself. That he chose the entire outfit and not just the socks as a protest item to assert his autonomy.

"Try holding your hands still and a little bit lower," I said, wanting to add, Little Man, to the end of my tip.

He didn't look at me but he did what I said—the water spurted out of the faucet, he rubbed his hands together beneath the flow and then wiped his hands on his pants before leaving. I liked that he didn't say anything to me, no gratitude or prickly response because I told him what to do, and that he didn't even acknowledge me, not a glance or a nod. But I could almost hear his voice in my head: I'll do it like that next time too, hold my hands still, hold them closer.

I glanced at my reflection and caught myself grinning like an idiot. When I stood up straight, I noticed that the headache was gone.

Chapter 3

As I exited the store, one minute after my shift ended, five over-enthusiastic guys ran past me. They were either hockey players or time-traveling cavemen—they had small foreheads that sloped down toward their eyes, bulbous noses, wide indestructible-looking jaws, bad haircuts that probably remain hidden from the sun most of the time by helmets or backwards hats or caves, and their bodies were swollen from whey powder and barbells. One guy, the lagger, bumped my shoulder with his, reminding me of Vince, a self-proclaimed cool kid in high school who used to walk down the narrow halls during class change and bump into everyone younger and smaller than him. It didn't hurt, but my head and torso spun back, my gaze landing on the group's struggle to get inside. The lagger, hit by the door swinging open toward him, stumbled back, almost toppling over, but regained his balance. I wanted him to fall on his ass and cry from pain and embarrassment. Then I saw him rub the shoulder the door had hit, the same one that he had bumped me with; I saw him wince while rubbing it and felt avenged. Three of the four guys in front of him looked back and laughed. "Wait up, fuckers," he yelled, running to catch up.

A new video game was probably released today, I thought, watching the scene and being reminded of Black Friday when everyone is out-of-their-mind stoked for hyped-up deals. Last Black Friday was my third as a salesman. Nobody got hurt that year—not at my store at least, but somebody somewhere got trampled because somebody always falls down and gets stepped on during the Black Friday stampede. The store had hired extra security last year because two bargain hunters were foot-squashed and hospitalized the year before. As if being flattened under boot heels wasn't bad enough, the shoppers, with footprints up their backs, didn't receive medical attention until after the first customers—the ones at the head of the pack who could work their elbows like an NBA player pulling down a rebound—had exited the store and called the paramedics. I didn't see the people but I pictured stout-looking hobbits, barefooted and hairy, weighed down with bags of cheap merchandise, scurrying to the exit and then calling 911 from the car as they sped off to the next store full of cheap goodies. If everything were just cheaper all the time, then nobody would have to kill each other for deals one day out of the year; they could kill each other every day of the year instead. I guess I shouldn't complain. I make my living selling thirty dollar cables that cost five cents to make, fetch fifteen dollars in commission, and should probably just come in the box with the device that requires them.

Part of me wanted to catch up to the guy who leaned his shoulder into me and stomp on his toes. But then I would've had to go back inside. No, he could have the game or whatever the group was jonesin' for. I was off and I wanted fresh air. I turned away from the store and took a deep breath—it felt like drinking ice cold water on a hot day. The air inside the store feels like the air of a plane at thirty-thousand feet: recycled, full of farts and halitosis. Sure, I might not be able to smell it all the time but sometimes I know that I just inhaled a fart and it makes me gag. It's like walking into a bathroom and smelling shit, ingesting fecal matter. I try to hold my breath and pop a mint afterward but if I've smelt it, it's too late.

Sometimes, when working, I hold my breath for a little reprieve, a recycled air vacation, but then I gasp and think that the fart air is getting into deep and seldom used parts of my lungs where it will build a home and fester until one day, when I'm sick, a coughing fit pushes the last puff of air out of the darkest recesses of my lungs and a stench cloud—made up of all the stink I have inhaled over the years—

escapes my mouth and knocks me out. I imagine it hanging there in front of my face, this green puff of putrid, this unearthly symbiont, mocking me before disappearing and moving on to inhabit another. Working in that place might have felt better if the air wasn't so stale. I'm sure the job causes my headaches—the air, the fluorescent lights, the top forty songs mixed with the hum of electronics and the cacophony of voices. I didn't get headaches before working there.

I took a deep glorious breath outside and gulped cigarette smoke. The annoying woman from Sunday's meeting leaned beside the entrance, holding a smouldering cigarette between two limp fingers. I exhaled, coughed dramatically, imagined putting out the cigarette in her eye, and kept moving. *Why do smokers have to stand right beside entrances?* Smoking should be illegal. Suicide is illegal, but smoking isn't. It doesn't make any sense to me. It's illegal to blow your brains out or hang yourself, which is relatively quick and causes no physical harm to anyone else—maybe some emotional harm for the person who finds your rancid, decaying body covered in shit, piss, and blood. It's legal, however, to slowly poison yourself with cigarettes, causing a world of cancerous, disease-ridden pain before you die a slow agonizing death and, if you're lucky, take some secondhand smokers down with you.

On my way to my car, I glanced back at the smoking waste-of-skin propping herself up against the building—*cigarette in eye, cigarette in eye, cigarette in eye, scream*—I'll admit it, the fantasy made me feel better.

Making my way through the packed parking lot, a cyclist flew past me in a streak of blue. I didn't even see him until he was right beside me. He tore through the lot, hopped up onto the sidewalk, and then down onto the street. After almost being run over by him, my first thought was of clotheslining him off his bike like a professional wrestler. As he rode away, oddly enough, I wanted to be him, streaking past cars and pedestrians, fearless and strong.

Watching him shrink smaller and smaller in the distance, I thought, *I could bike to work*. I had a bike, but it had been rusting in my parents' garage since the day after I graduated high school and got a car as a reward.

"Congratulations," my dad had said while shaking my hand, "for staying on the honour roll all three years, here's the car we promised you."

I used to ride that bike to and from school and work. Good exercise, fun. Not like cars.

I should start biking again. Maybe my bike still works or maybe I should buy a new one.

The cyclist disappeared. Before I got into my car, I looked up at the cloudless sky and took a deep breath. My eyes swam through the blue until I found myself searching for the moon, but I couldn't see it anywhere even after searching every inch of sky. It was gone.

"Are you okay?"

Looking toward the voice, I shaded my eyes with a hand. A plump, shorthaired, older woman stood by the open driver's side door of the lime green and black Smart Car parked in front of my beat-up Toyota. She looked at me like I was crazy.

"Yeah, I was just looking for the moon," I said, feeling silly.

"Oh," she said, her face softening. "There's a new moon today. That's why you can't see it," she said, smiling, closing the door, and turning away.

"Are you an astronomer?" I called after her.

"No," she said, "just a moon aficionado."

I watched the grey hair on the back of her head bob and move toward the store.

"Thanks," I practically yelled.

She turned and smiled. I got into my car.

On my way home, I decided to stop by the café where I had met Mercy on Sunday. I wanted to see if Amy was there. It was near the university and her place. She hung out there sometimes to do homework. On my way there, a woman was trying to drive her car up my tailpipe; all I could see in my rearview mirror was her car. I wanted to slam on my breaks and make her rear-end me; I always get that urge when someone is tailgating me. She looked down, probably getting something out of her purse, probably a phone, the perfect opportunity to brake. I imagined tires squealing, burning, smoking; metal crunching, bending, ripping; the rear-ender's face smashing against their steering wheel, blood spurting onto the windshield, teeth falling onto the floor mat.

While I watched her, my foot aching for the brake, I thought of the cyclist and how road rage probably never touches him. The woman sped out from behind me, flew past, and cut me off while holding a phone to her ear and laughing maniacally. When I have to work, road rage is kind of a good thing because it gets my blood pumping and the pent up anger makes me a better salesman. When I'm angry, I don't feel bad about selling people junk they don't need. When I'm on a road rage high, I enjoy taking people's money. Fuck 'em. I'm mad and the more I shove into my pocket and the pocket of the store the better. After my anger subsides, I wish I could give the money back—it feels dirty somehow. When I'm spending it, I feel ... nothing.

We came up to a red light. I squeezed the steering wheel, my knuckles turning white. Then I let go and rolled down my window. A few deep breaths made everything okay. The music coming from the car beside me with all its windows down helped. I could hear the song perfectly. I'd never heard it before, but it made me tap my foot on the brake, the taillights of my car probably flashing on and off as I tapped.

The woman in the car beside me was swaying to the music and singing along, her lips wrapping around every word as if she'd written them herself. She was the singer, drumming her right hand on the steering wheel that was her microphone, her red hair so bright it seemed to be glowing under a spotlight. I wanted to be her passenger. I wanted to sing with her, but I didn't know the words.

Just then the car in front of her lurched forward and she followed suit. The song faded as she pulled ahead of me. I hummed it until I couldn't remember how it went anymore and then turned on the radio to look for another tune.

"... Officials say that the extent of the destruction from the natural disaster is not yet known, and according to the helicopters on the scene—"

I changed the station:

"... And now, for all you baseball fans, we have the scores from last night's games—"

Another station:

"... The flooding is reportedly the worst in 50 years …"

Another station:

"... We have two tickets for tonight's concert for the first caller who can give us the—"

Another station:

"... Our resident gardening expert has stopped by the studio today to give us some helpful—"

Another station:

"... Said today that the additional healthcare cutbacks are a necessary measure to avoid deficit spending—"

Another station:

"... Make your way to a dealership nearest you for this limited time offer—"

I shut the radio off. My phone vibrated; it was Mercy again. I used driving as my excuse not to answer it. He probably wanted to borrow my car early, to have me meet him at my parents' house. As my phone vibrated, I pictured Mercy sprawled across my parents' couch in his underwear, drinking beer, watching a football game or sports highlights. The thought of walking into that house and seeing him lounging, his haggard ball sack escaping from his shorts and sticking to his inner thigh made me glad I didn't answer.

I could almost see the OLIVE LEAF CAFÉ sign a few blocks away. I hoped Amy was there. I also secretly longed to see the barista again, her pierced bellybutton that was somehow not trashy at all, blue eyes I could get lost in, and her contempt for Mercy, like a siren song luring me to the café.

Chapter 4

Amy was the first person I saw when I entered the café. She sat alone at a table with three empty chairs, holding a glass of orange juice to her mouth with one hand and holding a book open on the table with the other, her eyes fixed on the ceiling as she drank. She had dyed her hair since I'd seen her last, a dark red almost the colour of dried blood. It suited her. She could have been born with that colour. I walked toward the bar observing her, I wished her roots would stop growing so she could always wear that shade as her own. Amy's hair was shorter too, her new style a cross between bed head and toque head. She looked intelligent, bitchy but fun if you got to know her.

"What can I get for ya?" the barista asked.

It was the same girl that Mercy hit on when I was there before. She gazed at me with eyes that could swallow me whole, so I looked past her at the menu on the wall behind her because that's what people do, because I didn't want her to realize that I was there for her, because in her eyes lay my own embarrassment. I didn't want to be lumped in with Mercy, just another jerk who tried to pick her up. I glanced back at her eyes and there was no recognition.

"Just a water, please."

She passed me the ice-filled, sweating glass. I thanked her and moved over to Amy's table. Amy stared down at her book.

"Excuse me, hot stuff, should I sit here or on your lap?" I made my voice sound a little deeper than usual and started pulling out the chair beside her without waiting for her to respond. She slowly lifted her head, her eyes closed and probably rolling beneath their lids.

"Excuse me," her hand gripping the glass tighter as if she wanted to throw its contents in the intruder's face. Her cold gaze and sharp grey eyes turned soft as she recognized me.

"Hey," she said, laughing and pushing on my shoulder. "I thought you were some jerk. What are you doing here?"

"I came to see you."

"How'd you know I'd be here?"

"Lucky guess. Your hair looks really good."

"Oh thanks." She ruffled her hair with her fingers while smirking and looking at me. "I did it last week."

"It suits you." I looked around the café. "How long have you been here? Has Mercy stopped by?"

"No. Why?" she said, her expression turning grave the same way it used to when Mercy was trolling the house looking for someone to torment. "Is he coming here too?"

"Relax. He's not meeting me here or anything."

She sighed. "Thank God. I really can't take him today."

"He's just been calling me, so I wondered if he'd come here looking for me."

She leaned back and crossed her arms. "What does he want from you now?"

"To borrow my car," I said, smirking.

Amy laughed through her nose and shook her head. "He's unbelievable." She leaned forward, furrowed her brow like a kindergarten teacher about to scold a student, and cut her hand through the air in front of her, a gesture that almost knocked over her OJ and sent orange flying up into the air before splashing onto the table. "Why doesn't he …" She steadied her glass. "… just borrow Mum and Dad's car. It's practically his anyway?"

"I don't know. Because he's Mercy."

Amy wiped up the spilt juice with her napkin. "Let's not get started on him. We could go on for hours." She sighed and leaned back. "How are you? How's work?"

"Work. How's work? Well, I thought about stabbing a coworker with a pen during a meeting last Sunday." I took a sip of water.

"That good, huh?"

I laughed. Water almost spurting out my nose. "Yeah," I coughed. "That good."

"Do you remember when Mercy stabbed the Henderson kid in the leg with a pencil?"

"I totally forgot about that," I said. Images of Mercy sitting on a chair in the middle of the kitchen and getting yelled at by my dad filled my mind. "Are you stupid? Do you have any brains in your head?" my dad shouted. "That's enough," my mum snapped back, as close to yelling as she ever got. Then she sent Mercy to his room.

"Didn't Mum and Dad make him apologize?"

"Yeah," she said, "but they should've made him see a shrink. Maybe he wouldn't be so messed up if they had."

"It wasn't that bad."

"Not that bad," Amy scoffed. "It's the kind of story people tell about serial killers when they were little kids. The reporter asks, 'Did he have any violent tendencies as a child?' and then the mother or whoever says, 'Well, he did stab another boy in the arm with a pencil once.'"

I laughed but wanted to change the subject. Joking about your brother needing therapy and having serial killer tendencies shouldn't be funny. But it was funny, and I felt guilty for laughing because there was some truth to it; I didn't want to contemplate how much truth.

"Well, anyway, I didn't stab her."

"I'm glad to hear that you're not just like Mercy."

I thought of Dan and Kurt and became consumed with an overwhelming desire to quit my job. Or just never go back. "One of my managers told me I'm not selling enough warranty. And the other manager told everyone to forget about their lives when they come to work because he doesn't give a shit."

"You should really quit," Amy said.

I took a sip of water.

"Or at least drink something stronger than that to get through it."

She was right. I either had to quit or become an alcoholic. Unsure which path to take, I turned my attention to her book. "What are you reading?"

She showed me the nondescript cover of a huge hardcover and said, "It's your Henrik Ibsen book."

"I thought it looked familiar. Do you like it?" I sat up and leaned forward, wanting to rip the book out of her hands, to read all the plays again. "Have you read *An Enemy of The People* yet?"

"I'm reading it right now, but I just started."

"It's great. It could have been written yesterday."

"It's good so far," Amy said, nodding as if she'd just opened a Christmas present and gotten socks.

"Well, I love it and I'm glad you're reading it. After you're finished that play you should read *Ghosts.*"

"Is it good?"

"It's great. It might be my favourite play."

"I'll read it next, but this thing's huge," she said, lifting up the book to show its weight. "Ugh, I can barely lift it let alone read it."

"Just read those two," I said, gently taking the book from her. "You know I recommend books to Mercy all the time, but he never reads them." I flipped through the pages, my eyes catching a line or two that I recognized. "He'd rather read magazines."

She grabbed the book out of my hands. "The day Mercy reads a book is the day I move back in with Mum and Dad." She flipped back to her page and started reading again.

The door to the café opened—I turned. A man and a little girl entered holding hands. They made their way over to the bar where the man ordered a coffee to go. I could only see his profile while he stood at the bar waiting; he kind of looked like Rob Lowe from the side. Then I noticed the little girl stood facing me. I smiled, but her expression remained neutral as her eyes explored my face. She didn't seem to care that I was staring right back at her. I wondered what she was thinking. *Wouldn't that be a great superpower to have? The ability to know what people are thinking when they look at you?* But I had no power over her. She had a power though, that little girl. Something others don't have. She seemed wise and fearless, able to do anything, to be whatever she wanted. Maybe we're all like that when we're little, but when we grow up we lose it. I wondered if I had the gift she had. If people saw it when they looked at me. She seemed perfect standing there looking at me, just being and being content just to be. The man took his coffee and tried to lead the little girl toward the door; she didn't move, so he said, "Come on Emma, let's go." Then she turned to follow him but she kept looking back at me until the door closed off her gaze.

It's weird how dogs aren't supposed to be eye contact animals. Apparently they will only glance into people's eyes, alpha dog stuff or something like that. Kids are the opposite; they look right in there. It's as if they're trying to see your soul. Maybe that's why some people like dogs so much and hate kids. Dogs do what they're told; kids want to know why.

Amy was still reading when I turned back to her. "How's school?"

She wedged her bookmark in between the pages. "It's fine. I have lots of work to do so I'm here, reading something that has nothing to do with school. It's just hard to get into it sometimes." Jolting upright a little she said, "Oh, I almost forgot. Could you help me install a program on my computer?"

"Sure. When?"

She squished up her face like a little kid begging for candy and said, "Now? I need it for this project that's due next week."

"Yeah, let's go."

Normally I don't like it when people ask me to help them with their computers because it happens all the time, but I was willing to do anything that allowed me to procrastinate calling Mercy back. And it was Amy. I liked doing things for her even if they were my least favourite things.

"Great. I just need to hit the loo before we go."

Amy went to London for two weeks last year with one of her classes and has called washrooms loos ever since. She also came back saying water closet and underground and tele and give him a ring and that's brilliant.

As she disappeared into the WC, I downed my water and took the empty glass to the bar. Sitting on a stool, I noticed the music playing throughout the café. It was toe-tapping good and sounded really familiar.

The barista stopped wiping the counters and took my glass. Her hair was tied up and behind the few strands that fell lazily over her eyes, I could see her pierced eyebrow. It made her look rough, even sexier. She wore another tight belly shirt but this one was black and said, CREAM OR SUGAR in white letters across her breasts. "Do you want anything else?"

I wanted to be her shirt but I would've settled for being the writing on her shirt or just one strategically placed letter. I tried to keep from staring at her chest but the letters were begging for it. "Yeah, could you tell me what song this is?"

"Sure, hang on a sec." She turned and grabbed a CD case from a shelf. The top of an indiscernible tattoo poked out from under her collar. It could have been anything. I sat up to try to see more of it but she turned back around with the antiquated CD case in hand, cutting off my view.

"Whoa, what's that?" I said, pointing to the CD case.

"I know, right?" she said, handing it to me.

"I don't remember the last time I even held one of these."

The CD case felt strange, light and delicate.

She flipped the case over in my hands, so I could read the list of songs on the back. Tilting her head to the side and pointing, she said, "It's called 'White Collar Boy.'"

"It sounds similar to a song I heard on my way here."

"It's a sign. You should go buy some of their CDs." She smirked and leaned against the counter on her forearms.

Don't look at her breasts. Don't look at her breasts. Don't look at her breasts.

"Do you like this band?"

"I love them," she said, sounding much less like a robot programmed to take drink orders.

I wanted to keep her talking but my mind went blank. She let her hair down, scrunched it with her hand, and slid the elastic onto her wrist. I wondered how her hair smelt, how it felt, how her skin tasted.

"I should probably buy the album."

She pushed back from the counter, "Do, okay." Her tone changed. "Buy them I mean." She sounded like a cop threatening to give me a jaywalking ticket. "Don't steal them off the internet."

"I won't. I, I don't pirate music."

"Cool," she said, smiling and relaxing again.

I smiled back and felt like I was about to blush.

"I mean, I used to when it was a new thing but I haven't for years."

"You ready," Amy said, appearing behind me, adjusting the bag strap on her shoulder.

"Uh, yeah." But I wasn't ready. Not even close.

I held out the case.

The barista took it from me and squinted slightly. I had no idea what that meant so I waved and said, "Thanks." I felt like she was watching me and Amy as we left, but she probably wasn't.

I should've gotten her number. Mercy would've gotten her number. No, she probably would've turned him down. She might have given it to me though. Mercy just wanted her for her body; he didn't care about what music she liked.

The entire walk to Amy's I thought about the barista. Amy told me all about the program she needed help with, but I had to get her to tell me again once we were in her apartment because I hadn't retained a single word.

"It's a design program," Amy said, a little annoyed at repeating herself.

"Right. Sorry." I sat down at her computer and began rummaging for the disc, moving clumps of paper around. "So where's the disc? I'll have it ready to go in two minutes."

Amy put her bag on the couch. "Well, the thing is, I don't exactly have the disc."

I turned to her; she was giving me that please-don't-be-mad, I-really-need-your-help cutesy face. "What do you need?" I asked.

"Could you just get it for me? Please?"

I laughed. "Just procure it out of thin air you mean?"

"It's like a three hundred dollar program that we're supposed to buy for school," she said, more than a little upset about it. She sighed. "School's a fucking rip off. So," she began, her smile growing in spite of the resentment she felt toward the university's penchant for bleeding students dry. "I thought you could get it for me for free instead." Amy smiled so big that her face lit up like a jack-o'-lantern.

I lined up my fingertips on the home row of her keyboard and said, "What's the name of the program?"

It was downloading within minutes.

"Thanks Felix. You're the best." She disappeared into the kitchen. "You want some apple juice?"

Amy had this amazing organic apple juice that was just about the most refreshing drink on the planet. I did want some. As she got drinks ready in the kitchen, I noticed university letterhead poking out from beneath a pile of papers on her desk. I pulled up on the sheet of paper to reveal more of what was written beneath the seal:

Dear Amy Bowman:

I am writing to you, Amy Bowman (ID: 1167549), regarding your assignment entitled "Marketing Your Business Today for Tomorrow's Clients" that you submitted for MARK 368 on October 1, 2014. It has been brought to my attention by Dr. Sandro Sabat, your Business and Marketing professor, that there is concern your essay may contain plagiarized material. Plagiarism is defined in section 30.1.7 of the Code of Student Behaviour as follows:

Plagiarism is the misappropriation of—

"What are you reading," Amy said, emerging from the kitchen with two full glasses.

"Nothing," I said, shuffling the letter to the bottom of the pile and then taking a glass from her.

Her movements noticeably slowed. "What?"

I shrugged. She reached into the pile and grabbed the letter, glancing at the words on the page before looking at me again.

"This is nothing," she said, tossing the letter onto the top of the pile and then taking a sip of juice. "I forgot to cite a couple sources." She put her free hand on her hip. "Sabat's an idiot. I'll meet with the Dean, she'll wag her finger at me, and I'll plead ignorance."

Standing above me, looking down with her one hand on her hip, she looked just like Mum when she was about to engage in a wee bit of scolding. Both hands on hips was reserved for full-on disciplining. I took a long, hard sip, wishing I could dive into the glass and swim away. She was lying, but I didn't want to get between her anger toward Sandro Sabat and her defensiveness; I did feel compelled to ask her if she needed my help with anything.

"No," she said. "Don't worry about it. If it was serious, you'd be the first to know."

I nodded and glanced around her place. The knot tightening in my gut told me it was serious, but I stopped my concern from bubbling up and out my mouth in an accusatory tone that would only make the angry mum side of Amy lash out.

Her apartment was a small one-bedroom with a lived-in mess. It looked like it could use some renovations or at least different flooring and a paint job. Carpet's the worst. Especially old carpet because it has countless years' worth of filth festering in its fibers. If carpet could exhale and cough up the layers of grime choking its furry lungs, anyone nearby would suffocate on its phlegm. One of the main reasons why I chose my apartment was the laminate flooring; it's cheap and scratches when the wind blows too hard but at least it's not carpet.

I chugged the juice. I just couldn't stop drinking once it hit my tongue. "Oh, that's good," I said, putting down the froth-coated glass, and panting like a little kid who still hasn't learned how to breathe while drinking. "Damn that's good juice."

"Yeah, I love it," she said, turning to her computer. "How long will it take?"

"A couple minutes to download and then I just have to install it."

"You're amazing with computers," Amy said. "I have no idea what I'm doing."

"Well, I work with them all day."

The realization depressed me, so I searched for some kitten videos while we waited for the program to finish downloading. We laughed and awwed and then the program was done.

As I installed it, I wondered how the barista felt about pirating computer programs. I had a feeling she didn't care. She seemed like more of a music lover than a software nerd. After it had installed, I clicked on it, it opened, and Amy stood up and hugged my head.

"Thanks Felix. You're awesome. Now I can finally finish that project."

She's a hugger, which isn't always a good thing, but this time it was. I was surprised how much I needed a hug, even a goofy head one. It reminded me of the time my finger almost got ripped off by the heavy Caravan door when our whole family went on a mission to buy Beanie Babies. When we got to the mall I was so excited that I slammed the door on myself. My bloody finger made my whole body throb and tears explode from my eyes. We had to go to the hospital instead of inside to get the toys. I remembered Mercy whining about not getting his toy the whole ride to the hospital. I tried to stop my finger from bleeding, to clot the wound just by willing it so that everyone could go back to having the day that they had planned. My finger throbbed harder and harder the closer we got to the hospital and the farther we got from the mall. Amy hugged me all the way to the hospital and helped me hold the wad of fast-food napkins over my finger. I cried the whole way. The next day, everyone went out again, but I stayed home because I didn't want to screw everything up again. Amy came home with her cute, soft little Beanie in one hand and the one I wanted, Tabasco the Bull, in the other. She handed him to me and then hugged me so tight my stitches almost popped open.

She took control of the mouse and started clicking around the program. "If I wanted to install this on a friend's computer, how would I do it?" she said without taking her eyes from the screen.

I noticed the index finger on her free hand picking incessantly at her thumb. It was a weird tic I had never noticed before. *Probably just anxious about her assignment*, I thought. So I showed her the files she needed to copy and the READ ME file that explained how to make the program work without a key.

"Thanks," she said. "You'll have to show me how to pirate stuff one day. Then I won't have to bug you to do it for me anymore."

I said that I would and then stood to leave. I was tired and didn't want to be around computers for the rest of the day. Before I left her apartment, she told me she'd make me dinner to repay me. I told her not to worry about it, but she insisted.

Walking back to my car, my mouth started watering at the thought of Amy's cooking. She was a great cook, and I hadn't had someone cook for me in a very long time.

Chapter 5

On my way home from Amy's, I passed a church—its lawn was full of people dressed in black. It must have been a funeral. Women wore dresses. Men wore suits, some with jackets and ties some without one or the other. The kids looked just like the parents, only miniature. As I drove by, gawking at the people, I saw a little girl all dolled up. She stood alone on the road with one foot in the gutter, jumping in a small puddle of water, her white leotards splattered with dirt, her arms stretched out like a bird's wings, her little fists clinging to her velvet dress. When she jumped, she pulled the dress up and when she stomped down in the murky puddle, she pushed it down. She looked like a flightless bird flapping its wings, jumping, her feet sending filthy gobs of gutter water into the air each time she failed to takeoff. She stared down until I got closer, and then she looked right at me. I could see muddy splashes on her face, neck, and all over her Sunday best, her knowing expression the same as the little girl's in the café.

In my rearview mirror, I saw a priest take her hand and guide her out of the puddle and off the road. He leaned down and whispered something into her ear, and she ran back toward the church. *What did he tell her?*

Was it about God and how He likes good, clean, virginal little girls? Would she tell others what he had said and then would they tell others like this huge game of telephone that completely distorts the original message?

I remember playing telephone in grade nine drama class. There were probably thirty kids in the class, and we all sat in a circle, which was really a beat-up oval, while the teacher whispered the original message into a student's ear—it was always a little suck-up next to the teacher, the pet who would whisper exactly what the teacher had said into their neighbour's ear. The whispers went around and around from student to student. I was usually somewhere in the middle. One time I stood next to Jose—a boy well beyond puberty who could have been my dad's mechanic—and he whispered, "Turtles begin wanting quiet time," into my ear. I remember how bad his breath smelled, like Nutella and garlic chili fries, and how I could almost feel his five o'clock shadow, at ten in the morning, on my cheek. I passed the message on as I heard it even though it sounded wrong. Sometimes it's fun to throw a totally different sentence to the next person but there seemed no need with that message. When the message returned to the source and was whispered into the teacher's ear, she repeated it out loud, "Hurtles being wet quit the mine."

Everyone giggled at the absurdity of the sentence. Then the teacher told us what the original message had been: "True acting begins with quieting the mind." We all laughed at how much the message had changed, at how, incrementally, we had all distorted it.

Seeing the priest whisper something to the little girl made me think of the telephone game, where words morph, meanings change, and I'm left not knowing what to believe. So I just don't. And then I laugh.

Chapter 6

My apartment building reeked of seafood, curry, pizza, scrambled eggs, bacon, garbage, and macaroni and cheese all spewed into the giant barf bag that was the porous hallway carpets. I got a little nauseated making my way toward my door on the third floor of the walkup, through the jungle of stink, my hand and arm swinging like a machete to cut a path through the thick, odorous vines surrounding me. When I stepped inside my place and closed out the stench, the comforting smells of my life massaged my nostrils—a hint of vinegar from the floors I had recently mopped, garlic and tomato from last night's pasta, wet dirt from plants I'd watered the day before, dirty dishes lingering in the sink, and the hint of rotting garbage.

I hung my keys on the hook beside the door and looked around. Everything was just the way I had left it. No matter how many times I check the burners and the oven to make sure they're off before I leave—three to five times depending on how many forgotten items send me past the kitchen again—I'm always happy to come home to find that my life hasn't burned down. I usually touch all four burners before leaving just to make sure. But after I lock the door behind me, doubt wraps its suffocating hands around my throat—I either missed checking one or didn't touch the burners long enough to determine whether they were off or on.

Thankful my place wasn't a charred remnant of my home, I stared into the living room; a few dust particles floated and danced in the sunbeams glowing through the glass of the patio door—they made me think of fish playing in a fish tank, free but trapped, dead if out of the sun.

Stepping into the kitchen, I glanced around at the dirty dishes littering the sink and counters and I wished a magical, dishwashing fairy would have appeared from somewhere beyond the world of frolicking dust while I was gone and cleaned up after me. I always tell myself not to let dishes sit because, whether mouldy or covered in petrified food chunks, they're harder to clean the longer they sit. Yet I always leave them and have to work ten times harder than if I would have just washed them right away.

The first dish I grabbed, a plate, was about a week dirty and alive with mould. Watching the spores spreading their decay across glass, I contemplated washing it and then realized that I'd rather eat the black banana on top of my fridge, peel and all, than scrub the dishes, peel and all. I had other plates anyway. That is, after all, why I have so many dishes. I can go for weeks, and I often do, without washing any. Sometimes I even stack dishes on the fridge because I run out of room in the usual dirty dish stacking places. When I run out of clean dishes, I consider tossing all the dirties and just buying new cleans. That's what rich people do when the maid quits I'm sure. I'd just be playing it rich.

Reaching inside the fridge, I grabbed a pot of leftover pasta, a big wooden spoon sticking out of the pot. I sat on the couch, put my feet up on the rest, and ate the cold pasta right out of the freezing pot with the huge red-stained spoon. I liked the way it felt to drag my teeth along the spoon. The wood, so soft and vulnerable, reminded me of chewing on my pencil in school. I swallowed a sliver of yellow once in grade six; while nibbling on my well-gnawed pencil, a shard slid to the back of my throat and down. For the rest of the week I could feel it in my throat even though it had probably already been flushed down the toilet. Tasting the wood of the spoon, I felt the ghost of that pencil sliver; my throat remembered it and hated me for it.

As I licked the spoon clean after my first few bites, my pocket began vibrating. I knew it was Mercy before

I even looked at my phone. Putting the pot down on the cushion beside me, I answered it.

"Hey buddy," Mercy said. "Buzz me up."

"You're downstairs?"

"Yeah, let me in."

The hand holding the phone dropped into my lap. My head fell back and hit the wall. "Fuck," I said, a harsh whisper that escaped my mouth like an exasperated gasp. I glanced at the pot of cold leftovers beside me then to the phone in my lap and wished that I had no way to buzz him up, wished such a convenience hadn't been attached to the nine digit on my phone. Not wanting to buzz him in, wanting him to rot in the lobby as punishment for just showing up without calling first, I pressed the nine on the number pad as hard as I could in hopes that he'd feel my thumb pressing down on him. Then I squeezed the phone like one of those stress balls and wanted to chuck it at him when he strolled in and went for the fridge, which I knew he'd do. Mercy is the king of unannounced lobby calls. He makes me feel like a stranger in my own home, as if whatever I have will always be his.

Staring at the unlocked door and waiting for it to open, my head began to throb. I rubbed my temples for a moment before pulling a migraine pill out of my pocket. Then I took a spoon full of pasta, masticated it unrecognizable, popped the pill into my mouth, and swallowed. Surprisingly, it was easier to take it with food. The thrill of this discovery wore off quickly when I looked at the door and could hear his footsteps coming down the hall. I wanted to hide or leave, but I just sat there until he entered my place as if he were coming home.

Mercy could stroll into a stranger's house, make a sandwich, watch TV, take a dump, not flush, and write, I WAS HERE, on the wall in black marker, thinking nothing of it. He sauntered into my place and went straight for the fridge.

"Don't you have any beer?"

"Guess not," I said, giving him the finger through the wall that separated the living room from the kitchen.

The fridge shut. I lowered my finger. Mercy emerged and walked over to me, sitting down on the footrest my feet were on, forcing me to move my feet in a hurry before he crushed them with his muscular hockey butt.

"Do you ever think about calling first?"

"Hey, when did you get this footstool?"

"What? I don't know. A couple months ago. Why?"

"How much was it? It's nice."

"I don't remember."

"I like it," he said, bouncing up and down on it like a little kid.

I closed my eyes and sighed, listening to the stool squeak under him. "So what's up?" I said, opening my eyes and trying to sound emotionally authentic, like I didn't care.

He leaned toward me and spun his cap backwards, his widely spread legs on either side of my crossed legs like the mouth of a predator closing in on its prey.

"So say a friend of yours asked you for a favour. Would you help them no matter what?"

"Is this hypothetical?"

"No! I don't want you to guess."

"What? No, hypothetical not hypothesis." *You idiot.*

"Huh?"

"Is the situation real or made-up?"

"Both."

"Okay." I didn't know how it could be both but I said, "Well, tell me the situation, and I'll tell you what I'd do."

"That is the situation. A friend of yours turns to you for help. They came to you over everyone else, and they need your help."

"That's all I get?"

"Yep."

"Is it illegal?"

"It could be. It could be anything, but it isn't as easy as lending 'em five bucks."

"How strong is the friendship?"

"It's strong, okay. Just answer the question," he said, like an impatient child.

"You're not really giving me enough to answer."

"C'mon. It's not that hard."

"How can I give you an honest answer when I don't even know the whole situation?"

"You know everything you need to know." He leaned forward on his elbows. "A friend needs your help. So do you help her no matter what?" Mercy turned his hat around and pulled the brim down just above his eyes.

Wanting him to leave so that I could finish my pasta and go to bed, I said, "I don't know."

"Just say the first answer that comes to you."

"That is the first answer."

"Well, what's the second?"

"I … I don't know what I'd do until I was actually in the situation."

"Just tell me what you'd do."

"Fine. I guess … I would."

"You'd what?"

"I'd help them if they needed me."

"No matter what?"

"I don't know about no matter what but I—"

"Ah, come on."

"What? You don't like my answer?"

"No, it sucks."

"I told you that I'd help, but the consequences of helping would really determine if I would or not, okay." Sometimes it felt as if we spoke different languages. Instead of trying a different form of communication, Mercy just keeps saying the same thing louder and louder until he's yelling in my face as if the louder he says something the better I'll understand it.

"But what if the help is worth any possible consequence?" Mercy said.

"Does this have anything to do with my car?"

"Maybe," he said, shovelling a spoonful of pasta into his mouth and then getting up to sit in the chair beside the couch.

"If you don't tell me what you're gonna do with *my* car, you're not borrowing it." I pictured my car flipped over and on fire, Mercy laughing psychotically, pissing on the flames while watching the wreckage hiss and pop.

"Don't worry about it," he said, his mouth full of my food. He stood up and went to the kitchen. I could hear him rummaging through the cupboards. "Want some gin?"

"I'd rather know what you want with my car."

"It's no big deal," he said from the kitchen, the sound of ice cubes hitting glass cutting his words to pieces.

Mercy came back sipping from a glass and holding another.

"What are you gonna do?"

"Help a friend." He held out a glass.

"Murse, just so you know," I took the glass, "you're paying for whatever happens to my car."

I took a sip. It was strong but good, the gin I had in the back of the cabinet above the fridge. It filled me like a long meditative breath. I couldn't even be mad about him helping himself. Mercy should always be served with alcohol; I wanted to chug from the bottle.

"Are you gonna tell me what's up? What friend?" I finished the drink and sucked an ice cube into my mouth.

He stood, grabbed my glass, and went back into the kitchen. "Maybe after another," he said. Ice cubes hit glass again. "You said you had Monday off right?"

"Yeah. So …"

As I sat there, my eyes began to itch; I rubbed them until they watered. The sensation turned me into a ten year old again, lying on the floor of my parents' TV room with my eyes closed. Mercy had told me to close them, had walked up and stood above me with his hands behind his back. I thought he had an awesome big-brother present for me so I did what he asked. When he said, "Okay, open your eyes," I opened to see the salt and pepper shakers rocking up and down in his hands right before my slow-focusing eyes began to burn. My eyes were instantly on fire. I flailed around on the ground crying and screaming for my mum, rolling on the ground as if my entire body were engulfed in flames.

My mum appeared, "What did you do?" she asked Mercy as he laughed uncontrollably.

"He shook pepper into my eyes," I cried.

"Go to you room," she told Mercy. "This isn't a funny joke."

I tried to open my eyes to look at Mercy, but air felt like flames on my exposed eyes. I could only hear him giggling and his foot steps moving upstairs to his room. Mum led me to the bathroom. She helped me flush my eyes with cold water, asking me why Mercy had done it, what game we had been playing.

As I waited for Mercy to make more drinks, I felt as if I was lying on the floor with my eyes closed—just waiting to feel the sting, my eyes itching in anticipation.

The next drink was even smoother than the first, stronger too but refreshing in a way that made my whole body sigh. The next was even stronger.

"So I ah," he snickered, "got maced the other day." He finished off his drink and slammed the glass down on the floor.

Liquid flew out of my nose. "What?"

"Yeah." He got up to make another drink and spoke up from the kitchen. "So this girl was all over me in the bar, right." Poking his head around the dividing wall in the kitchen, he said, "I mean, she even stuck her hand down my pants while we were dancing."

"So why'd she mace you?"

"I have no idea, man." He stepped back into the living room, moved the pot of pasta to the footrest, sat down on the couch beside me, and poured half of his mammoth drink into my glass. "We went outside to fool around in the alley and then she freaked out and sprayed me."

"Jesus, man. Did it hurt?"

He shook his head. "Not really. I mean she missed me and hit the wall so that might have been why. But some bounced off and splashed in my eyes and that kinda hurt." Mercy took a sip. "The full spray would probably feel like having your eyes scratched out."

"I think that's the point," I said. Finishing off my gin, I wished the girl would have gotten him right in the face, and then I felt as if I'd put her up to it, as if I'd manifested this payback by just remembering what he had done to me. Or maybe it was the whole karma thing that made it happen.

He sunk deeper into the couch and rubbed his eyes in a moment of sensory déjà vu. Mercy seemed defeated and small for the first time since I watched him break his hand on his opponent's helmet while his hot blood rained down from broken cartilage onto ice —the ice soaking up the red like a sponge before fusing with the blood in a frozen mess.

"You all right?" I asked.

"Yeah, no big deal."

"C'mon. You must have done something. Nobody breaks out mace on a whim."

He shrugged. "I just returned the favour," he said before polishing off his gin.

"What does that mean?" I got up and fixed us both another drink.

"I stuck my hand down her pants."

Well, then you deserved it you prick, was my first thought when I walked over to him holding our drinks. *But mace, wasn't that a little harsh? And hadn't she started it? According to Mercy she had but who the fuck knows? I guess she knows. The mace knows.*

"Did she say anything before? No or stop?" I said, passing him his drink.

"Just the mace freak out. No biggy though."

I didn't know what to say; I was stuck somewhere between *good* and *that's too bad*, so I just drank.

Mercy chewed up an ice cube and smacked my shoulder playfully. "It's too bad too, 'cause she's shaved."

And I drank some more. He had deserved it. I didn't speak for a while and neither did he. I had nothing to say to him, and he didn't seem to have anything to say to me. The silence stretched on until he grimaced, switched his glass to his left hand, and then slowly extended his right hand wide before making a fist. He did this over and over.

He glanced at me as he exercised his hand. My expression must have looked like a gigantic question mark because he said, "It's nothing."

I finished my drink, refilled, and brought the bottle over. Mercy downed his last sip and refilled.

"You still playing hockey?"

"Nah," he said, shrugging.

"Is it because of that?" I said, gesturing to his hand.

He took a swig and then hissed air in through clenched teeth.

"You used to love it."

"Yeah. I still do. I just …" he stopped himself and stared down at his glass.

I stared at him—he looked like someone had let half the air out of him. For the first time, I noticed stretch marks on his biceps, biceps that were clearly not as swollen as they used to be. I wondered if he had the marks—which looked like little scars clustered together—elsewhere, if all his muscles had started to recede. Mercy's mouth hung open, and I decided that I would sit there quietly until whatever he wanted to say finally came out. He wasn't a fast thinker. He was a fast doer.

I couldn't remember the last time we sat like this, brothers, on a couch, drinking, talking sort of. It felt foreign but there was something comfortable about it too. He had saved me once, from Eli York. It was in grade ten. I was rushing to class because I had slept in and missed my bus. I rode my bike as fast as I could that day, but I still arrived five minutes late. Sweating, fumbling with my books as I ran around the final corner to my class, I collided with Eli York—a twelfth grader with ears on the verge of cauliflowering from three years of rugby, who always wore his short sleeves rolled up to display his massive arms, and was notorious for injuring opposing players on the field; once an ambulance had to cart away a kid with a broken collarbone while Eli, grinning like a sadist, accepted pats from teammates and never took his eyes from the kid writhing with pain from grass to back of ambulance. When play resumed, Eli seemed to be hitting even harder than before, jacked on adrenaline and glee.

We didn't see each other, Eli and I, not until chocolate milk dripped from the tip of his nose, soaked deep into his white T-shirt, my books lay on the floor lapping up the pool of brown milk seeping from the carton next to them, and Eli's closed fist squeezed the life out of my unsullied shirt.

"Why don't you watch where you're goin'?" he said through clenched teeth.

I couldn't speak. I didn't say sorry or anything. I just tried to walk away as if he weren't holding me there. That's when he dried his hands and face on my shirt, smearing chocolate all over it. Then he let go, staring at me like he wanted to eat me. I bent to pick up my books, and he said, "You're lucky I have another shirt in my locker."

I didn't respond, occupying myself with gathering my books and shaking off as much burnt cream as I could. When I stood up, Eli was right in front of me blocking my way whichever direction I turned. He grinned with collarbone-breaking delight, licked his lips, and said, "After school, behind the gym. And don't try to run away because I'll just have to chase you down and stomp you into the ground." Then he smacked the side of my head twice and disappeared around the corner. After that, being late for class didn't matter. I wanted to cease existing, to vanish, or to go back in time and count to ten before rounding that corner. Instead, I went to the office, told them I wasn't feeling well, and called home. I didn't think about my parents being at work, about Amy and Mercy off doing their own thing. I just called home, and Mercy answered.

"Hello," he said, breathing heavily.

I could picture him in his underwear, glistening with sweat, the handles of his dumbbells warm at his feet. "Hey," I said.

"What's up? I'm kinda in the middle of somethin'."

"I don't know."

"What do you mean you don't know?"

"I wanna come home."

"So come home. I don't care."

"Can you pick me up after school?"

"No. Take the bus. I'm busy."

"But ..."

"But what?"

"... Eli ..."

"What about him?"

"... Never mind."

"Whatever. Are you finished?"

I hung up without saying anything else.

"Your mum or dad coming to get you, darling?" the secretary with the small-town accent asked after I had hung up the phone.

I shook my head.

"Do you have another shirt to change into?"

I nodded. "My phys ed shirt."

"Well, go on and change into that and then head straight to class."

Sitting through classes for the rest of the day in my gym shirt, I could feel where the sticky milk had dried on my skin. I avoided all my friends so I didn't have to tell them about Eli, ate my lunch in a bathroom stall, and stared at the clock, wishing I could stop time. When the final buzzer of the day sounded, I put everything in my locker and stepped outside. The entire rugby team was behind the gym, in their cleats, mouthguards in or hanging out of their mouths, ready to practice. I saw Eli York right away—what was left of his ears were tapped back with a band of white tape around his head; he jumped up and down bringing his knees into his chest. My heart was pounding in my throat. I saw Coach Macnair walking toward the group of Neanderthals, his arm around one of them, and my heart slowed. There was no way Eli could touch me with Macnair around. I felt my body relax and bowels try to release. Then Eli turned to face me. He grinned, the top row of teeth black from his mouthguard.

"Eli," I heard someone call from the group.

Eli turned away from me, and then I saw Mercy emerge from the pack. He was the one the coach had his arm around, and I didn't even notice. Mercy bro-hugged Eli, said something I couldn't hear, and then walked toward me. Eli grinned at me again. Mercy looked at me then turned back to Eli and pointed at him.

Mercy walked right past me and said, "You comin'?" over his shoulder. We drove home with the stereo of his '89 Mustang blasting, the windows down, and our arms out in the open air. He never told me what he said to Eli York, and I never asked, but Eli never touched me again.

As we sat there in silence on my couch—Mercy searching for the words to describe why he didn't play hockey anymore, a sport he claimed to still love—I almost wanted to ask him about Eli.

"It's this," he said, knocking on his head. "Too many concussions."

"How many have you had."

"A few."

"And they won't let you play anymore?"

"I stopped playing years back," he said, leaning forward to top up his glass." He took a gulp. "Right after my scholarship got cancelled."

"I didn't know you had one."

"I didn't even tell Mum and Dad." He sunk back into the couch and looked up at the ceiling. "Yep, full ride to go to school and play. But that was what … eight, nine years ago now." He sniffed hard and finished his drink. "I could've been a university type like Amy," he said, chuckling. "Can you picture that?"

I shrugged and smirked. I didn't know what to say.

"Pisses me off thinking about all of that university tail I missed out on," he said, turning to me, his eyes wet. He chuckled again, and his right eye began to leak —he stopped the droplet by cutting his hand across its path. Then he picked up the pot of cold pasta again and started eating.

Should I hug him? No, it's too late. Maybe pat him on the leg or something. No, he's eating. He's already moved on.

"This is good," he said. "Even good cold." He put the pot down and filled his glass.

"Felix?"

"Yes?" I said, in a cautious tone, never liking what came after Mercy said my name.

"I have a serious question now so don't laugh." He leaned forward and turned my way, his forearms just above his knees propping him up.

"Okay."

"Would you kill me if I asked you to?"

"Sure."

"No, seriously. If I was in an accident and gonna be a vegetable for the rest of my life or if I was, you know, suffering and shit because of some uncurable disease. Would you?"

"What? Kill you?" I said while thinking, *it's incurable, dummy*.

"Yeah."

"Hmm, would I pull the plug you mean? ... If you were dying?" I munched what was left of my ice cubes, the sound of crunching ice so loud in my head that I couldn't think for a moment. It was such a random question.

"Yep. Dying."

"And there's no chance you'd get better?"

"Nope."

"And it's what you want?"

"Yep."

"Then yeah, I'd do it."

I took a sip.

"Good," Mercy said. "I'd do the same for you."

"Good. I don't wanna live if I can't live. Nobody should have to live if they don't want to. And if they can't do it alone then ...."

"Shit yeah. They're our lives. We can do what we want with them."

"Hey, if I were drowning, would you throw me a life preserver?"

"I'd toss you a fucking life raft," he said.

"Of course you would. You don't go small. You'd toss me an island if you could."

"Or jump in after you."

"See? It's the same thing," I said. "Pulling the plug and not letting me drown. People think they're different but they're the same, you know."

"Right. Wait. How?

"How what?"

"How is pulling the plug on someone—" Mercy belched "—the same as saving them from drowning?"

"Because … because it's like … drowning on a disease right. On an illness. And the life preserver, the fucking life raft … is the plug."

"I still don't get it."

"You see it doesn't matter if you're throwing a raft or pulling a plug or … or saving a life or ending one, okay. It doesn't matter. 'Cause, 'cause it's helping someone. It's doing what's right. It's saving someone pain and distress."

"Damn right," he said, raising his glass and taking a sip.

"It sure as hell isn't selling them computers. Am I right?" I tried to take a sip but got only gin-flavoured melted-ice water. "And morality doesn't depend on, on if somebody lives or dies. What's moral is what's right. And what's right is ... is ..."

"Helping someone when they need it," Mercy said.

"Exactly. Quality of life matters. Not just life."

The acrid taste in my mouth made me want to hang my tongue out of my mouth so I didn't have to taste it anymore.

Quality of life matters. Quality matters. Quality. Quality.

My life seemed suddenly empty as my own words rattled around in my head.

I could have done anything.

You sell computers.

I could have been anything.

You sell fucking computers for a living.

What am I doing?

What does it matter?

I think I need to puke. Where's my fucking plug to pull? My parents lied to me. I'm a failure. Why'd they tell me I could do anything?

You can't be anything. You are a failure.

Mercy slammed his glass into mine. "I'll drink to that," he said, taking a swig.

I stared at the glass in my hand, wanting to feel compelled to smash it on the floor but instead felt indifferent to the glass's existence and my power over it.

"I need you to come with me on Monday," he said while gulping down the last of his drink.

"What? Where?"

"To see Lisa."

"Who's Lisa?"

"A friend."

"Okay."

"Did I ever tell you about her?"

I shook my head; it was light and bobbing, my eyelids sticking together when I blinked. One more drink and I would have gotten the spins; I put my glass down on the floor and pushed it away from myself.

"We went to the same junior high and high school," he began, "but we weren't really friends until later. I always liked her though even though we never really talked or anything. She was one of the hot girls, you know. I asked her out once in grade eleven, but she turned me down. She turned everybody down. She just wanted to be friends. Why do girls always say that? I thought if we spent enough time together we'd eventually end up screwing."

"What's her name again?" I was intrigued by this mystery woman who turned him down.

"Lisa."

I closed my eyes and nodded. *Lisa. Lisa. Lisa.* The darkness behind my eyelids was a big comfy pillow I wrapped my arms around and snuggled into. Mercy shook me. His hand felt like a bucket of cold water jolting me awake.

"Hey. This is why I need your car."

"Okay, I get it."

"No, you don't. I haven't told you everything."

"What more is there? Did you finally get to sleep with her?"

"No," he said, raising his voice.

"Okay. Sorry. So we're going to see her so you can. I get it." I just wanted to lie down on the couch and pass out. I leaned toward the armrest and tried to curl up. "I get it."

"No no no no no no no," Mercy said, pulling me back up before I could lift my feet onto the cushion. "You can't sleep yet. I have to tell you something."

"What?" I opened my eyes to look at him but he was really blurry.

"We're going to pull the plug on her."

"What?" I said, rubbing my eyes to focus them.

"She has cancer."

"What?" I shook my head to try to wake up.

"She's had it forever. As long as I've known her. And she's done."

"What are you talking about?"

"We're gonna help her."

"She's done? What does that even mean?"

"That she wants—"

"Hold on. We? When did this … how am I … I never said I'd—"

"Shut up for a second, and I'll tell you."

The couch rocked like a boat. I gripped the armrest and cushion to try to stop the stomach-churning motion.

"She's done all the treatments. She's not getting better. And now she's done. Okay? She's just done."

"You keep saying that, but what does it mean?"

"She wants to die. She's ready. She's had enough, and I promised I'd help her."

"You promised you'd murder her."

I couldn't think of how the conversation got to this point, who Lisa was, or why I drank so much. My head started to throb again.

"It's assisted suicide, asshole."

"Oh, I'm the asshole?"

"Yeah, you're the asshole."

"Right." I thought the booze was causing hallucinations. I hoped it was. It had to be. I pressed the heels of my hands into my eyes until I saw stars. "Go home," I said, as if that would stop the pounding in my head, stop Mercy from saying anything else, stop the motion and the taste of death in my mouth.

"Not until you say you're in."

I lowered my hands and looked at him, little flashing lights all over him. "In for what? Up to fifteen to twenty-five years as your cellmate? No thanks."

"What happened to what you said? The right to die, blah blah blah, and all that?"

"Those sound like pretty important blah blah blahs."

"You just said that saving someone and pulling the plug were the same fuckin' thing. Remember? The same thing 'cause it's helping. And helping people is what's important. What happened to that, huh?"

"Oh, God." I flopped down head first on the couch.

"What about that?"

"That was when it was hypo-fucking-thetical. You're talking about killing someone. Do you even realize what you're saying?"

I covered my eyes with a hand, the lights were blindingly bright.

"Yep, I do."

"Don't say *yep* like you're going to help her paint her toenails."

"Well, what do you want me to say?"

"That you're kidding."

"Well, I'm not."

"What about jail? Are you willing to go to jail? Is it on your fucking bucket list? Murder and spend time with inmates. Check."

"Stop saying that. Jesus. It's not murder. I'm not going to fucking shoot her."

Reclining made me feel worse so I stood and started to pace slowly, like a ninety-year-old man who shuffles instead of steps.

"You don't even know what you're saying."

"Yes, I do."

"Then you're an idiot," I said, standing still to look at him.

He shook his head and looked just like Dad, pissed about his favourite mug shattered on the kitchen tile, disappointed about a lousy report card in his hands, sickened at how I didn't know something he considered to be obvious. I snatched my glass off the floor and went to the kitchen sink. I poured and downed two glasses of water and then filled my glass again. Mercy was still on the couch when I walked back, his arms stretched out on the top of the cushions forming a gigantic T shape with his body.

"Feel better?"

"No."

"I have to do this."

I took a sip of water.

"I promised her. That's it."

"Well, that was dumb."

"You're such a hypocrite."

"You're a hypocrite."

He laughed. "Whatever. Are you in?"

"Why'd she ask you, huh? Out of all the people in the world, why you? Doesn't she have any friends?"

"It's just meant to be."

I choked on my spit. "You think it's fate or something?"

"Yeah."

I laughed, louder than I expected. It was full of contempt and anger, of pent-up rage that had never surfaced before.

"She knew I'd do it."

He sat up straight. I kept laughing.

"That she could count on me and no one else."

"It's not fate," I said.

"It is."

"It's not." My knees seemed to disappear. I sat down on the couch because I thought I'd fall. "It's not."
She picked you 'cause you're stupid enough to do it.

"Are you in?"

"No." I poked my numb face a few times with an index finger and stared at the ceiling. The stucco was moving, like distant clouds forming recognizable shapes that disappeared before I could name them.

"Why haven't you mentioned Lisa before? This friend with cancer?"

"I thought I had."

"Nope. Not even once. Not even half of once."

He told me about all the random girls. All the ones he had 'banged.' All the one-night stands, even the ones whose names he couldn't remember. He even told me about that paraplegic girl he knew back when he was still into speedos and baby oil and still dreaming of glistening in front of judges as he flexed beneath floodlights on stage. He told me about how he used to lift the paraplegic girl out of her wheelchair and carry her places. Then, as if he got what he wanted from her and dropped her, he just stopped talking about her.

"How come you never told me about Lisa?"

"I don't know. Are you in?"

I couldn't keep my eyes open. I reclined on the couch and this time Mercy didn't stop me.

"So what if you get caught?"

"I won't."

I snickered. "Okay. That's probably the one thing inmates forget to say and think before breaking the law."

"I won't get caught if you're watching the door."

I sat up as much as I could but couldn't open my eyes even though the darkness was spinning. "That's what *in* means."

"C'mon. We're brothers."

I felt like throwing up, on him, in his face, projectile bile that burns flesh and corrodes bone. To him it was my duty to do whatever he wanted. He made being brothers feel like something to be ashamed of. I lay back down, floating closer and closer to the spinning black. "Doesn't she have any sisters or best friends that can help her?"

"She's an only child, and she asked me. Are you in? C'mon. Watch my back for me."

"You know, you have no idea how to ask for things. You're a demander. You never ask. You never say please. You never ask. 'Let me borrow your car.' You see. 'Watch my back.' Where's the please? Where's the thank you? You know Murse, a little courtesy goes a long way. Remember that."

"Please, Felix."

"Please what?"

"Please help me do what's right."

"Why is it right?"

"Because she has an uncurable disease. 'Cause she's suffering. And 'cause of what you said before, helping someone who needs it is what's right. Saving someone from pain is what's right. And Lisa, Lisa's drowning, man. She needs us to help her."

The last thing I remember saying before I passed out was, "The word is *in*curable."

Chapter 7

That night, I dreamed of Mercy.

We sat facing each other at a small round table in the Olive Leaf Café. He talked and he talked and he talked, his mouth never resting or pausing, never halting to gasp for breath as if his life depended on his mouth forming words rather than taking in oxygen. He wasn't frantic about it though. The only frenzied part of him was his mouth; he sat slouched with one leg up on the table, the dirty sole of his boot inches from me. I stared at the perpetual movement of his lips and jaw, hearing nothing. We were in a silent film without subtitles; I leaned forward and squinted at his mouth as if I'd be able to read the words on his lips, but his lips moved too quickly, flapping like an auctioneer's whose life depended on the sale of an excessively priced item, his desperate words vanishing as they formed.

I held my coffee cup, which was frozen and painful to the touch even though steam rose from the molasses-black liquid inside. I held it as if it were warming me through, and began to shiver, shivering harder the more I squeezed the cup in search of heat. When I raised the mug to drink—resolved to keep my gaze fixed on Mercy's lips—each sip tasted like 100% dark chocolate, an impossibly bitter saliva thief that slid down like peanut butter, clinging to my throat, almost expanding as it moved down.

I added sugar in between sips using one of those glass cylinder white sugar dispensers with metallic lid, pouring with one hand and stirring with the index finger of the other. The coffee never got sweeter. My finger, stained black.

Mercy didn't drink anything, but as I watched his incessant talking and sipped on the sludge that was my coffee, I thought of his hatred for coffee. He turned to sixteen ounce energy drinks for his in-between beers drink. He drank coffee only once. When he was nine and the babysitter called, "Bedtime," down the basement stairs—her voice carrying into the far end of the basement where we sat cross legged on the carpet staring up at a 45 inch rear-projection TV that displayed the blood and carnage of the video game we played. Mercy snuck up the stairs, into the kitchen, and grabbed the half empty coffeepot off the maker before disappearing into the bathroom—he locked the door behind him. Old, cold, and bitter, the coffee had been sitting there all day, the dregs of my parents' morning pick-me-up. The babysitter pounded on the door until Mercy emerged, holding his stomach, breathing deeply through his retching mouth, the blood drained from his face. In bed that night, I fell asleep to Mercy's whimpers.

Drinking my cup of goo, I could feel my face turning the same sickly green colour as Mercy's had that night. I needed to get rid of the drink but, for some reason, couldn't dump it out. So I chugged and I gulped, trying to finish the coffee with a final effort, choking at the last minute and sending an entire mouthful of black flying across the table. The black hit Mercy in the face and his mouth finally stopped moving. I felt like the dinosaur that blinds its prey with sticky goo in *Jurassic Park*. Dripping down his face and onto his chest, the liquid looked more like coffee, but the black ooze that suddenly began dripping from the sole of his boot beside me was more like tar.

Laughter exploded from my mouth and echoed through the café. Everyone looked at us. I laughed with coffee dripping from my nose, and Mercy sat there stunned—his hands, in loose fists, dangling in front of him like those of a punch-drunk boxer.

Chapter 8

I woke up to the start and stop hum of my phone vibrating with an incoming call—the rattle of the phone amplified by the cheap coffee table it scuttled across. I opened one eye to find that I was on the couch. Mercy was gone, but the pot of half-eaten pasta was still on the footrest beside me. I watched the phone buzz closer and closer to the edge of the table, the entire apartment seeming to rattle and move with it, my head—congested with hangover pressure—inching closer to the edge of the couch cushion precipice. Reaching out to silence the racket, I knocked the phone onto the floor. The phone hit with an ear-splitting thud.

"Fuck," I groaned, flinching from the clunk.

Suddenly more awake, both eyes open, I glanced down at the phone, display down on the floor. My heart began to beat slightly faster as I imagined my phone's smashed display kissing the wood, lips of a thousand shards that would next kiss my fingertips and draw blood. I propped myself up on an elbow and reached—the display was fine but the vibrating had stopped. I held my thumb against the button: TRY AGAIN appeared and shook back and forth at the bottom of the display. I tried again and again until the phone prompted me for my code. My code didn't work either. TRY AGAIN now a permanent fixture on the top of the display above the numbers. Confused, I turned the phone over in my hand and, this time, noticed Mercy's case. It made the phone look like an old-school mixtape. I reached my free hand down to grope the outside of my pocket. I fingered for the hard rectangle but felt only thigh. Mercy had taken my phone by mistake.

"What an idiot," I said, sitting up straight, my heart thundering in my chest and head. Then my hand instinctively fell to the outside of my other pocket, discovering my phone slumming it in the opposite pocket for a change. I pulled it out and sat for a moment with fists full of phones. My heart slowed back down to it's alcohol-poisoned—*whump, whump*—pace, with the occasional palpitation.

I tried my thumbprint on my phone; it unlocked and had no new messages for me. I then turned back to Mercy's phone and tried his birthday date—TRY AGAIN. Then I tried the year he was born—TRY AGAIN. Then I tried pressing 1 four times, and the phone unlocked to reveal a blond in a thong bikini, sitting backwards on a metal chair, her ass, back, and profile taking up the entire screen. I rolled my eyes, and said, "Of course," my voice raspy and sounding as if it came from another room, from another person. I cleared my throat, swallowed, and double tapped the fingerprint scanner. The phone displayed all of Mercy's recently used apps. I thumbed through them until the photos app stopped me—a video was queued up, a big play button floating over a freeze frame of a distorted closeup of a woman smiling. I tapped the app and then play.

"Come on," Mercy's voice came through the speaker. "You've done it a hundred times. Just let me record it once."

He kept trying to thrust the camera into a woman's face for an extreme closeup, but she tossed her head from side to side to stay away from the lens, her auburn hair glowing like fire in the sunlight as it flipped back and forth hypnotically. Glimpses of soft skin appeared, and I wanted to touch it.

"Okay," Mercy said. "I'm putting down the camera."

The camera swung down in a blur of motion and settled on black. Gin remnants gurgled in my throat, and I had to close my eyes and breathe deeply to keep from puking.

"Just do the thing with your tongue and then I'll closeup on it," Mercy said. "Okay? Ready? Lisa tongue show, take one."

I opened my eyes to the black screen.

"Fine," she said, her voice somehow soothing my stomach. She sounded calm but firm like a teacher with the hint of coquettishness.

The camera flew up, and she looked right at it, looking slightly unimpressed, her fair skin glowing in the sunlight, her pink lips glistening after she licked them, her piercing blue eyes threatening to break the camera lens.

A single word escaped my mouth in a whisper, "Lisa."

She feigned a glare before sticking out her tongue— it looked like a clover with three leaves. Mercy moved in for an extreme closeup; the camera couldn't focus; all I could see was moist pink, and my cock seemed suddenly more sensitive to the cotton pressed up against it.

They laughed, Mercy's nauseating cackle balanced out by Lisa's sweet giggle. Then a blur of motion again, and the video stopped. I zoomed out so that I could see thumbnails of all the photos and videos on Mercy's phone. Flicking through to find more of Lisa, I came across countless selfies of Mercy with women of all ages, shapes, and sizes. Sometimes they were kissing his cheek, other times they were kissing each other, flashing some skin, duck facing it up for the camera, mostly in bars, mostly glistening with alcohol sweat and too much makeup or not enough. Then I found another video of Lisa: she sat on grass, wearing skinny jeans and a plain white tank top, her knees up, arms wrapped around them, chin on arm. She smirked at the camera, raised a hand to her mouth, and closed her eyes as she kissed her hand and blew the kiss to the camera. I reclined and watched it once, then again and agin. There wasn't any talking, just the muffled sound of wind hitting the microphone. She looked beautiful and serene with her eyes closed, sitting there quietly on the grass. I watched it one last time and then looked for more videos. There was a series of photos of her, probably captured in burst mode. She stood in front of a fountain and then spread her arms out like a dancer, shifting her weight to one leg and kicking her othcr lcg out to the side. It was captured like stop motion for the one perfect picture in the middle of the sequence where she looked like a professional ballerina with superb balance and form. And then she fell forward frame, by frame, by frame, laughing in the final few photos, hands on her knees, both feet planted firmly on the ground.

I found another video and hit play. It was of Mercy dancing in a dark club, surrounded by people. The jerk and sway of the video made my stomach turn. I stopped it, put down the phone, and looked off toward the bathroom, the room spinning a bit. I squeezed my eyes shut and then noticed the taste in my mouth—an acrid combination of garlic, tomato, booze, sleep—and my stomach went rancid. The sun yelled through the windows at me, ricocheting off the laminate floor, hot and almost blinding. My head throbbed like a fingertip hit with a hammer, and my tongue clung to the roof of my mouth like a leech.

I'd endure bloodletting if it would take away the pain.

The smell of the old pasta and the taste in my mouth, now like curdled milk, stirred the sludge in my stomach. Two deep breaths seemed to settle the bubbling that reached up to my throat. Rolling off the couch with a thump, desperate for water, toothbrush, and shower, I crawled to the bathroom on all fours— being low to the ground made the world easier to take. Once, I stopped to press the sides of my face against the cool floor, one, the the other. It felt like a cold washcloth on my feverish skin and reminded me of how my mum always used to give me a cool washcloth when I had a fever.

My phone rang and vibrated in my pocket. I took it out and left it on the floor as I continued my trek to the water closet. It continued to ring and vibrate and seemed louder than ever in the hall.

When I stood up in the bathroom, my head felt on the verge of cracking open. It was as if my brain had had a growth spurt in the night and now threatened to crack through my skull—the sudden ringing of my phone almost the impetus for the fracture. I shut the bathroom door to muffle the jackhammer-like ringing, stuck my mouth under the faucet, and drank until I couldn't drink any more. The mirror reflected my haggard face and the corduroy pattern of my couch imprinted on the side of my face.

After brushing and showering and swallowing a couple pills, I no longer wished for death to put a stop to the pain.

When the phone rang again, I picked it up off the hallway floor and answered it.

"Hey, how's it going?" Amy said, sounding a little too chipper.

I grunted in response and leaned against a wall.

"That good, uh?"

"I drank too much last night."

"I see. Well, no better cure than some delicious food. Wanna come over?"

"I don't think I can go anywhere just yet."

"That's cool. I'll come there."

"Food may not stay down right now."

She laughed. "What'd you do last night?"

"Drank with Mercy, if you can believe it."

"How was that?"

"I'll tell you later." I massaged my temples and then collapsed on the couch. "Listen, can I call you back later?"

"Sure. But you're getting a meal sometime today. How about tonight?"

"Okay, tonight's better. Wait, shit. I work."

"After work?"

"Okay, I'll call you tonight. Bye."

"Wait a sec."

"What?"

"That program works awesomely, and I finished my assignment. Thanks. You saved my life."

"I thought you were going to say I saved your bacon."

"Have I ever said that?"

"No, but now I want bacon."

"Gross. Anyway, thanks."

"Hey, anytime you need me to steal software, just ask."

"Have a nap and call me later."

I hung up and noticed that my car keys weren't on the hook beside the door. Mercy, the thief, had taken them. My heart began to pound faster and faster, my throat to burn. Lifting my phone in front of my face, I searched the internet for the formula to figure out my max heart rate and found a calculator to do it for me.

193? That seems like a lot, but I bet my heart rate is over. It has to be.

Dropping my phone onto the cushion beneath me, I closed my eyes, placing my left hand on my chest and two fingers from my right on the pulse point on my neck.

Will it stop? If it goes over, does it just stop beating? I don't want to die. But I can't stop it.

You're just hungover.

Fuck that. My heart has never raced like this before. Something's wrong.

Nothing's wrong. Relax. Breathe. You'll be fine.

I am breathing.

Sporadically.

Fine.

I started to take slow, deep breaths.

Is that better?

Much. Count to five in and again to five out.

I'm already counting my heartbeats.

You're feeling your heartbeat, not counting.

This isn't helping.

You're not counting.

Fine. I'll count. 1 ... 2 ... 3 ... 4 ... 5 ... It's still not helping.

It's helping.

What the fuck do you know?

What do you know?

That something's wrong.

Then call an ambulance.

I'm not calling an ambulance.

Why not? You need medical attention.

I don't know if it's that bad.

You were dying a moment ago.

Yeah but ... this breathing is helping I think, and my hand on my chest is too.

So you're okay?

I think so.

Good.

What was that?

Why are you asking me?

Don't you know?

Don't you?

Lying there, my heart slowed as I continued to breathe and count and breathe and count. I kept my hand on my chest and wrapped my arm over my eyes to block out the light. I breathed and counted and breathed and counted.

Are you still there?

...

Did you abandon me?

Behind my eyelids, I stood on a pitcher's mound in a crowdless stadium. At home plate, a poised batter and catcher were the only other players on the field and both waited for me to pitch the ball in my hand. I wound up to throw and followed through, but the ball didn't leave my hand. The batter tossed his bat and trotted to first base, removing his batting glove along the way and tossing it to the ground. Another batter appeared. Then another and another. Again and again I tried to throw the ball but it never left my hand. Bats were piling up beside the mound. The bases were loaded now, and the harder I tried to throw the ball, the more points the opposite team scored by simply walking across home plate. The catcher stood up and lifted his mask onto his head so he could yell at me, his face turning blood red, spit flying out of his mouth. I looked down at the ball and then turned my hand over —the large red stitching, sewn into my flesh, curved over and around the back of my hand. The catcher yelled louder and louder. I wound up and threw as hard as I could. This time my hand and the ball flew through the air before striking the catcher in the face, knocking him down and out. My wrist spurted blood. I touched the stump to my cheek; the blood, hot and wet, ran down my face like tears.

Chapter 9

I woke up to Mercy, standing above me, rolling a beer bottle back and forth across my forehead, the sweat of the bottle trickling down my cheek and neck. When I realized what was happening, I jerked my head away from him and the bottle.

"Wake up, buddy," he said. "I've got the cure."

I tried to take the bottle but my right arm wouldn't move, it was above my head and still asleep. Pulling my dead arm down with my awake one and placing it on my lap, I sat up, looking for Mercy's phone on the table —it wasn't there. A junky-like panic started strangling me, I wanted a hit; the hunger almost made me puke and did make me start to shake. I needed that phone, needed to see more videos and photos of Lisa.

"Arm asleep?" Mercy said, dangling the beer in front of me.

I tried to take the bottle with my sleeping hand, but it was unresponsive, so I snatched the beer with my working hand, feeling the tingles of life moving through my empty hand. The beer, already open, sloshed a little on my pants. Mercy lifted another bottle, which seemed to have appeared magically, and clinked it against mine. More beer spilled onto my pants. As I stared down at the growing wet spot, he chugged, downing the entire beer in a few seconds. The sounds of his throat swallowing and then his lips smacking turned my stomach. When I brought the shaking bottle up to my mouth, the yeasty smell of the liquid inside forced my nose up and away from the mouth of the bottle. It wasn't what I needed. He had what I needed in his pocket. For a second, I thought I'd puke.

"Shakes too, huh. This'll help, man," he said, sitting down beside me. "Just drink it."

"I can't."

"How do you feel? Like somebody's punching you in the temples?"

"Something like that."

"Drink."

I pinched my nose and chugged the damn thing just to get him to shut up. It took me ten times longer than it took Mercy to chug a beer. I lowered the bottle and sat perfectly still for a moment, not sure if beer would explode out of me or settle within.

"You're still holding your nose," Mercy said, with a mocking smile.

I released my nose slowly, allowing the beer flavour to infect my mouth. Something began rising up my throat. I wanted to reach for something to throw up in but there wasn't time. I opened my mouth and a belch escaped; then my entire body sunk deep into the couch with relief. I sat still for a moment longer, wondering if more was on the way. Then my stomach turned violently and forced me into a dash for the bathroom. I could hear Mercy laughing as I watched beer spray into the toilet. When I stood up, after wiping down the porcelain with toilet paper and flushing, I actually felt better.

"Y'alright, buddy?"

"Yeah."

After swooshing and gargling mouthwash, I walked back into the living room. Mercy showed off by lounging on my couch and sipping another beer, the rectangle outline of his phone in his pocket the most pronounce thing about him.

"Feel better?"

I'd feel a lot better if you weren't here and your phone was in my hand.

"Much." I lay down on the floor beside the couch and closed my eyes, the yearning to watch more videos of Lisa ebbed a bit.

"Told ya."

Please just disappear again.

"Where'd you go?" I asked.

"To get beer and …," he rummaged through his pocket and pulled out a little bottle, "this."

"What's that?"

He looked at the label on the bottle. "It's … it's for Monday." He put the bottle back in his pocket. "So I figure we should be there at seven. Do you want to meet me there or should I pick you up?"

"What are you talking about?"

"You don't remember last night do you?"

I was trying to forget, to just not acknowledge anything, hoping that it would all melt away without ever having to be talked about again. "I remember. But this is your thing not mine."

"You said you were in."

"No, I didn't"

"Yes, you did. Remember? You watch the door. I go in. Give her this. We leave."

Did I? I wouldn't have. I shouldn't have drunk so much.

My brain was swelling, I couldn't think. "This is crazy, Murse. "I'm not killing anyone. And neither are you."

"You don't have to. You're just watching a door. That's all. No big deal."

"Doesn't she have a doctor who can do this for her?"

"No. She has us."

"I'm not going to jail for this. Now, if you want to rob a bank, that's a different story. At least we'll have money to start our lives over somewhere."

"I'm not joking."

"That's too bad."

He got up and sat beside me on the floor. "I'll be in and out in two minutes. All you have to do is make sure nobody comes into the room while I'm in there. Okay?" He patted my shoulder and then let his hand rest on me. "Okay? … You were okay with it last night."

"I was drunk last night and I'm pretty sure I wasn't okay with it."

He moved his hand to my chest. I opened my eyes to look up at him.

"It's fine," he said. "It'll be two minutes of your life. Watching a door and my back."

It was the first time he'd touched me like that, pleading and tender, kind and warm. It made me want to help him, to say yes. Say I'll do it. I'll protect you like you'd protect me.

Pushing his hand off me, I stood up. "I won't be an accessory to murder."

"No, man," he said, shaking his head, looking up at me. "She's killing herself, and I'm helping her. If anything, you're an accessory to an accessory."

"There is no accessory to an accessory charge. I'd be there helping you—"

"Relax okay. It's gonna look like natural causes. Okay?"

I looked at Mercy. I imagined him pinned face down on the hood of a cop car, red and blue flashing across his face, handcuffs locking his arms behind his back. Then the cruiser door shutting and thick glass separating him from the rest of the world. Then he was in a cage. Alone. And I couldn't visit him. Couldn't look him in the eyes and talk about the weather.

"Nobody'll find out. Just—"

"Why are you doing this?"

Mercy sat up straight and looked up at me, his face stretching long and relaxing into an expression of despair, an expression I'd never seen before. "Because it's her life, and she wants to take it," he said. "And everybody's acting like they own her life. Nobody else will help her."

As he sat there, helpless, my first impulse was to kick him in the face and watch the blood stain his skin. Then, I wanted to hug him.

"Please," he said. "Don't do it for me. Do it for Lisa."

"Shut up," I said, lowering my face into my clammy palms, pressing the heels of my hands into my aching eyes, the words almost a sigh.

"But I need to know."

"Fine. Just stop talking."

There was a long silent moment as I pressed harder and harder into my eyes. The pressure made strange lights flicker in the darkness, like the aurora borealis on the night sky of my mind. I wanted to open my eyes to only those streamers of light glowing through the darkness, directed by some invisible magnetic field, caused by particles bumping into each other.

"So, you're in?"

I nodded, keeping my eyes closed.

"Awesome." He stood up and seemed to be vibrating. The keys to my car were jingling in his hand as I heard him move toward the door.

"Where are you going?" I said, looking at him.

"I've gotta do a couple things before."

"When are you doing this thing?"

"Monday night."

I glanced at the keys and said, "Are you taking my car?"

"Yeah. I need it. Mine's still fucked."

"I've gotta work. I thought you needed it Monday?"

"Can you get a ride or take the bus?" he said, opening the door and taking a step into the hall.

"I guess so," I said, feeling like throwing up again.

"Cool. See ya Monday."

The sound of the door shutting felt like a knife cutting into the side of my head. I dropped onto the couch and buried my face into a cushion. Then I screamed until my throat nearly caught on fire and lay still in the aftermath of my muffled ululation.

I can't believe I gave in. My balls might as well be strapped into the passenger seat of my car because I certainly don't have them.

But what if he got caught because you weren't there? What would he take from you then?

I don't want to think about it.

Fine. Don't think. It's easier that way.

Fuck off.

Fuck on. You'll get better results.

How old are you?

How old are you?

Chapter 10

When I finally rolled over—embracing a cushion that was wet from drool—it was two o'clock; I had to work at three. Aside from a slight ache at the base of my skull, the hangover was gone, but I was hungry enough to eat the cushion I clung to.

I can't work. I need food and water and more sleep.

So call in.

Maybe I will.

Maybe you will.

I will.

You won't.

I'm going to. I have plans with Amy tonight anyway. I don't want to feel like this when I see her.

So what are you going to do?

I grabbed my phone, saw that I had three missed calls from work, and dialled the store's computer department number. As it rang, I wondered why they had called me and hoped Dan and Kurt would both be busy so I could just leave a message. A quick, I'm-not-feeling-well-and-can't-make it soundbite that could justify not answering their calls. My heart pumped hot guilt through my body as I listened to the *ring ring,* waiting to call in sick for the first time in my working life.

"Computer department," Kurt said, his nasal voice even worse over the phone.

I grimaced involuntarily. "Hey, Kurt," my voice sounded full of anxious phlegm, "It's Felix."

"Felix! Did you forget something this morning?"

My morning shift. I had totally forgotten. *Shit*. I wanted the store to blowup at that moment, killing Kurt and the conversation.

I sat up and said, "Sorry I ... I'm sick. I've been in bed all day."

Kurt sighed hard into the receiver, a loud and poisonous hiss into my ear. I winced away from the phone and then held it close enough to hear without touching it to my ear.

"You couldn't have called, oh I don't know, five hours ago to tell me? What's with you guys today. You're the third person to call in. Dan's pissed. Only Kyle called in before his shift."

"I'm sorry."

"Can you come in tonight?"

"I ah, don't think I can."

"Listen," he said, sighing again but this time more desperate than angry. "I'll cut you a break. I'm short-staffed here so if you come in until eight, I'll forget about you missing your shift this morning."

I wanted to hang up and pretend I hadn't called. Block all of the store's phone numbers and forget I ever worked there.

"Okay? Just help me through the rush, buddy."

I couldn't speak.

"Felix?"

"Okay," I said, the word forming on its own.

"Thanks, man. You're a real team player."

The receiver clicked in my ear, and I let my phone hand fall into my lap. Selling computers was the last thing I wanted to do and I had no idea how long it would take me to get there without a car. After grabbing an apple and a protein bar, touching all four burners on the stove three times each, I left my apartment. The key turned, the deadbolt extended, and I still had to turn the doorknob and push on the door three times to make sure it was locked.

The fresh air embraced me, feeling like a pep talk from an amiable but firm coach. *You can do it. You can do it. Now get in there and make it happen.* Nudged forward by a breeze, I looked around for a bus stop, realizing, at that moment, that I had never taken the bus to work before or even ridden a bus since high school.

Memories of bus travel began assaulting my thoughts —missing the big yellow tank and having to chase after it at full speed, cutting through backyards and a baseball diamond to make it to the spot where Marco got on; fighting with the amazonian Mary-Loo Pender in Grade Four; the expressionless zombies sitting on the blue city bus with their noses in books, eyes on phones, and ears plugged with music loud enough for everyone to hear. Once I upgraded to a car, busing was the last thing I thought of.

I knew there was as app to guide me, so as my phone displayed directions, I started to march in the direction of work. After waiting fifteen minutes for the Number Seven, it was going to take over half an hour to get there, only fifteen faster than walking.

I got to the stop. A hunched and broken old woman stood beside the bench waiting. Her posture was that of a person bending over to pick something up off the ground only she couldn't stand up straight afterward. She stared straight down at the sidewalk, turning her head to glance up the road every few seconds, scanning for the bus. I wanted to help her stand up straight or lift the invisible load that seemed to be dragging her ever closer to the ground. My eyes started to burn while looking at her, drying up instead of tearing. I pictured her lying in bed, her legs sticking straight up into the air while her back and head rested on the bed; I almost laughed out loud at the grotesque thought, my stifled chuckle escaping as a suppressed cough. I quickly turned away from her and started walking.

How does a person like that live? Day to day? Grocery shopping? Cooking? Walking without running into things?

The same way you do. Only it's much harder.

It's more than harder. It's practically impossible. How does that happen?

The same way other things do.

Could that happen to me?

Maybe?

Suddenly aware of my slightly hunched posture, I pressed my shoulders back and felt my spine stretch up. I felt two inches taller as I walked as fast as I could, trying to avoid looking like one of those ridiculous speed walkers whose hips turn and thrust and whose head clucks around like a chicken's.

My forehead sweat had started to bead and run down my face by the time I got to work. Seeing the entrance to the store only made me want to keep walking, to walk to the city limits and just keep going, to walk until my legs gave out or until I looked like that old woman who could barely stand anymore. But I turned toward the store entrance.

At the door with the word IN written in big red letters, people were streaming forward, past an aboriginal man who stood by the entrance with his cupped hands stretched out in front of him, his right pant leg torn in one spot up to the knee, his third-hand shoes bursting open in spots. He hopped from side to side as if on hot coals, as if the concrete had burned the holes into his sneakers. His bare toes hung out over the soles of his shoes like tongues and his dumpster clothes looked as if they'd never been washed. He made eye contact with everyone that passed and said, "Spare change? Spare change? Thank you. Have a nice day. Thank you. Have a nice day." Nobody gave him any money. Most people didn't even look at him. The man in front of me, wearing a suit and the kind of shiny shoes that curl up off the ground at the toe, marched inside without even glancing at the begging man.

"Thank you," the beggar said. "Have a nice day."

I wondered if, at that moment, the beggar questioned his own existence, if he asked himself, *Am I here right now? If not, am I dead? If dead, who will avenge me?* I reached into my pockets and put whatever change I had into his cupped hands, hoping the weight of the coins would let him know that I could see him.

He bowed his head and said, "Kind, sir. Kind, brother. Bless you. Bless you."

"It's really nothing. You don't have to—"

"It's something. Oh, yes it is."

We held each other's eyes for a moment and then he nodded, closing his eyes and leaning forward into a kind of bow. I nodded and moved through the door.

Inside, countless salespeople vultured around the store, circling customers and shrieking:

—Can I help you find anything?

—Do you need help with anything?

—Anything! Anything! Anything!

"Just looking," was the response even though most customers were about to buy something. All the salespeople could smell it on them, like blood to a scavenger. Making for the break room, I walked past everyone and all the merchandise, my stomach cramping from just being there. The air felt suffocatingly thick. Inside the break room, a few people sat around the large table, draped with a red bed sheet-sized table cloth, in the middle of the room; it was actually two of those cheap folding tables pushed together. While punching in using the computer in the corner, filling a locker with my stuff, and buttoning up a work shirt I had snagged from a rack by the computer, I thought about the beggar.

I gave him next to nothing. Maybe enough to buy a coffee and donut. I should have given him more. He shouldn't have thanked me.

You did more than others.

I guess but did I do it for him or me.

Both.

But what's he going to do with it? What can he do?

Buy a coffee and a donut.

To what end?

To live.

I locked the padlock on the locker and slipped the key into my pocket before stepping onto the sales floor. The aisles between rows of merchandise seemed narrower, the ceiling lower, the walls moving in on me. It reminded me of how I feel at my parents' house these days—a clashing of memory and reality that makes everything seem smaller.

A hand slapped me on the back, making me flinch.

"Oh," Kurt said with an uncharacteristic smile, "I didn't mean to sneak up on you." He put his arm around me and pulled me close to him. "I'm just glad to see you, buddy."

I had the urge to grab his arm and snap it over my shoulder, the sounds of hyperextension and cries of pain, to my delight, radiating throughout the store.

"There's this older couple over there that's been looking for half an hour. They won't let anyone in." He grabbed my shoulders and turned me toward the couple before giving me a little push.

I had to stop myself from growling, *Don't touch me.*

Shrugging away the trace of his touch, I stepped toward the couple.

"Full stink, Felix," he called after me.

Stop talking you little weasel.

They looked like a couple of retired newscasters, well-dressed and manicured for the public. They could have been in one of those retirement commercials that always portrays retirees as healthy, good-looking, and vibrant, with silver hair, good posture, and perfect teeth that look like dentures. They read the specs sheet of a computer on display, trying to figure out what the numbers meant.

"We need more than eight GBs of memory don't we?" the woman said.

They were tourists surrounded by signs written in a strange language, and I was going to be their overpriced guide, making everything so much easier and evoking a gratitude that overshadows the fact that they've been ripped off.

The computer they'd had for ten years probably just died, and I knew, before even talking to them, that I could talk them into anything. I smiled, stood up straight, and pushed the remnants of the hangover aside.

"You know, when I first started working here, I had no idea what any of this meant," I said, stepping toward them and pointing to the computer specs.

"We don't either," the lady said, smiling back.

"We know a little," the man said without smiling, looking down at his much shorter wife.

"It's actually pretty easy to wrap your mind around. I'm Felix by the way."

"Caroline," she said holding out her hand.

We shook and her husband said, "Chuck," holding out his hand.

"Nice to meet you. Well, the memory is like your short term memory: the more you have, the more you can do in the moment without the computer walking into a room and forgetting why it went in there in the first place."

They laughed. I smiled and continued saying what I've said hundreds of times before. "The storage is like your longterm memory. It's much bigger because it's for permanent storage, like filing cabinets. And the CPU is like the brain, the faster it is, the faster signals can be sent to the rest of the computer."

Kurt liked to compare computers to cars, but I, like most people, don't know anything about cars, hate the word piston, and have watched many customers just get more confused as he talks. I mean unless you're talking to a mechanic, it doesn't work. Imagine if doctors tried to explain a surgery that way, *We're just gonna pop the hood and change out some of your piston pins. And then after we rotate the tires, you'll be good to go for another twenty thousand miles.* Comparing one thing a person doesn't understand with another thing a person knows nothing about just confuses people. Kurt's an idiot. Analogies are stupid, but sometimes they break the ice and provide some clarity at the same time.

"Does that make sense," I asked.

They nodded.

"Are you looking for a new computer?"

"Our computer is a dinosaur," Caroline began. "We've had it for over ten years. We can't even check emails on it anymore. So we'd like a new one but don't know what we need."

"Or why this one's five hundred," Chuck said, "and that one's two thousand."

"Well, there are a lot of reasons for the price difference. But before we get into that, what will you be using the new computer for?"

The answers are always the same: email, google, banking, internet, internet, internet, she uses the thing not me, you use it for banking and checking stocks, but that's it, and email and your sports pool spreadsheets, well, I use it a little but you're on it all the time, you're on it as much as me, awkward smile and frustrated half laugh, furrowed brow and eye roll.

For most people, any computer will do. Hell, any smartphone will do instead of a computer. But nobody wants the cheapest model and only the early adopters and rich want the most expensive one. The second most expensive computer is what I mostly sell because

—

"It's a really fast computer that'll be able to do what you want now and do new, more advanced things if you decide to get into photo and video editing."

"Oh, I'm very interested in working with photos," Caroline said before turning to Chuck. "Remember that book Margret gave us?"

Chuck nodded.

"I want to make one of those for Brittany with pictures of Hector." She turned to me, beaming like a proud parent, and said, "We're newly minted grandparents."

"The only thing that'll limit you with this computer is your imagination."

There are only a few types of people who appreciate that line.

"We've got plenty of that."

And Caroline was one of them. When it comes to buying computers, people settle into only a few types: the in and out—knows exactly what they want, which doesn't include warranty, and is annoyed by the formality of purchasing; the waffler—has to come in and talk to a salesperson a few times about the same things before becoming comfortable enough to purchase; the crazy—surprisingly not covered in own faeces, in at least once a week, twitchy, no intention to buy, just in to pepper a salesperson with outbursts about government spying, eternal damnation, or obscure details about *The Lord of the Rings* movies; the douche bag know-it-all—usually in with a friend to contradict everything the salesperson says, lives in his parents' basement, and is only out because watching *Inception* again is happening Friday, always on Friday, and today's Thursday, not Friday, and the top spins at the end, and I know what that means, most people don't but I do; the old, sweet, and clueless—usually start looking because their old computer died, are not afraid to spend the money because it's been seven plus years since they last bought a computer, but afraid to buy the wrong thing, and have been nagged by their adult kids to 'get rid of that piece of junk and get a new one.'

I sold Chuck and Caroline the second most expensive computer in the store. Because it was the one I wanted. Because they could afford it. Because I hated that I was there and that they were there and that Kurt was watching me. I also sold them a huge display, a bunch of software, and all kinds of accessories. I even talked them into getting the technicians to set up their computer for them while they waited because for one hundred dollars they saved countless hours of their own time and patience. They bought full warranty, putting over three thousand dollars on Chuck's travel points credit card. When I walked outside pushing a cart load of stuff, Chuck led me to the car while Caroline talked about all the pictures of little Hector she had to get onto the computer. The beggar was still there, still hopping, still asking, still thanking. Caroline became steely and Chuck even more surly as they marched past the beggar while looking straight ahead.

"Spare some change. Thank you. Have a nice day. Have a nice day."

He thanked them for nothing. For ignoring him. I felt guilty about pushing the cartful, worth over three thousand dollars, to their BMW SUV. Maybe I should have talked them into giving money to the beggar instead. That would've been a hard sell.

I lifted the boxes and bags onto the leather seats in the back, shook their hands, and waved while they drove away. Then, I finally let the heavy smile droop off my face, my cheeks aching.

The beggar said, "Hey, brother. Spare some change?"

I stopped and looked at him for a second, and saw zero recognition in his eyes. "Sorry," I said. "I gave it all away."

"Good for you, brother. Have a nice day. Have a nice day."

When I walked back inside, I felt as if I had just run into an old high school friend who hadn't recognize me. I wanted to go back out there to say something, to ask if he remembered me, to take off my work shirt and ask him to look again, but then I heard Kurt's voice.

"Big sale, buddy. Big sale." He put his arm around my shoulder; it felt like barbed wire against my neck. "Full stink? Full stink?"

"Yeah," I said, "full stink."

He let go of me and clapped his hands. "Oh, nice work. One more sale like that and you can go home and back to bed okay? Okay? So, there's a woman over there looking at software. She needs a computer and I told her you'd help her." He slapped my back. "Go get her."

If he touches me again, I'm gonna break his fingers, I thought while walking to greet the customer.

"Hello," I said, putting on my heavy smile.

When she turned to face me and said, "Hi," my mouth fell open. "Felix. Felix, is that you?" Mrs. Shoemaker smiled before her hand flew to cover her mouth in surprise. "It's been ages since I've seen you. You look just the same. Well, older of course. More handsome. But just the same."

She looked exactly the same too. From her polka dot dress to her shoulder length bob cut. Her roots were grey though and the classes after mine had etched a few more lines in to her face, but it was her. Good old Mrs. Poobaker.

"So you're selling computers now?"

"Yes, I am. And are you still teaching?"

"Going on nineteen years."

As she nodded, her smile shrank and her eyes narrowed on me. I knew she was thinking about that day in class when I read out loud, the day she found out what everyone called her behind her back. I wondered if her students still called her that.

"So, how've you been, Felix?"

"Fine. Fine." I looked back at Kurt. He gave me the thumbs up and winked. I turned back to her. "You? How've you been?"

"Oh, you know. Same old, Mrs. Shoemaker." She pronounced her name 'Shoemocker.' I was pretty sure that was new. Poomocker just didn't feel as natural in the mouth. Poostalker on the other hand …

I had no idea what to say. "Want to look at some computers?"

"Yes. I know exactly which one I want."

"That makes my job easier."

She led me to the computer. "This is the one."

"Okay. Did you have any questions about it?"

"Just one."

"Shoot."

"How much can I get it for?"

"It's twelve hundred for the system."

Mrs. Shoemaker rolled her eyes. "I know how much the price tag says, Felix." She leaned in and glanced around. "But how much can *you* give it to me for?" she said, pointing at my chest when she said 'you,' her voice like a wink that could quickly turn into a glare.

I suddenly felt like Kurt's hands were all over me and I couldn't shrug them off. "Sorry but that's the price. We could look at a less expensive one if you want."

Mrs. Shoemaker's face hardened slightly. "Oh, come on, Felix. I know this isn't the real price. How much can you take off?"

"I can't take anything off. There isn't a lot of margin on computers."

"How about for old time sake?" she said, smirking like a coquettish school girl.

I wanted to slap her across the face. To see blood trickle from her nose. My heart pounded so hard that my throat began to burn. *Fuck you. Fuck you, you fucking bitch.*

"There are cheaper ones. Maybe we should look at those instead."

Her smile disappeared and she stepped back, straightening her posture. "Well." She cleared her throat. "I'm not paying more than a thousand."

"Then looking at one for $1300.00 probably isn't the best idea."

Red blotches grew on her neck. I moved over to a computer that was $899.00; she didn't follow. "This one might be perfect for you."

"No, I want this one." She glanced around the store. "Where's your manager?"

The last thing I wanted to do was call Kurt over so I said, "I'm sorry but these are the prices." She made some weird *psst* noise. As if I owed her something. As if I was the one being unreasonable. "This isn't a flea market," I said in response to the awful noise she made. "If you want to barter, you should probably go somewhere else." I was shaking now but not enough for her to notice. The tremble in my body made me feel unpredictable. I wanted her to leave before I started pelting her with insults.

Mrs. Shoemaker glared at me and then looked around to see if anyone was watching or had heard. "Fine I will," she said, raising her voice. And with that, she marched toward the doors.

"I'll never shop here again," she said to Kurt while fidgeting with her purse that kept sliding off her shoulder.

I watched her leave and wave her hand at the beggar to shoo him away.

Kurt was on me within seconds. "What happened? She was a sure thing. What did you say to her?"

"She wanted a 300 dollar discount. When I suggested a less expensive computer, she left."

His mouth hung open as he stared at the exit. "She'll be back," he said. Then he glanced around the store. "Go get another one." And patted my back. "One more and you can go."

Needing to get out of there as fast as I could, I latched onto the first person I saw, selling just a computer but with full warranty. Kurt loved the stink of it and let me leave.

On my way out of the store, I noticed the cash register drawer was open but the cashier was gone. I saw the beggar—still outside, still hopping with cupped hands—and glanced back at the drawer, at all the money. I looked around—nobody noticed me lingering by the exit. I reached forward and snagged a twenty before closing the drawer, crushing the bill in my fist and looking around again. I didn't think anyone had noticed but the cashier was walking back toward the till.

"Hey," I said. "You left your till open, so I just closed it."

"I did. Oh my God." She ran over. "Oops. I hope it's okay."

"I'm sure it's fine. Just remember when you're cashing out tonight." I shoved my hand, and the crumpled twenty, into my pocket.

"Thanks," she said. "Thanks a lot."

I left the store and put the twenty right into the cupped hands of the beggar. He stopped hopping and thanked me like I'd never been thanked before. He kept saying, "You're a good soul, brother. You're a good soul." I looked over my shoulder to see if the cashier was watching but she wasn't.

Walking away, the words, 'good soul,' bounced around in my head, making my chest tighten and burn and a throbbing pain radiate from my temples. I rubbed my chest but the fire inside only grew, squeezed my neck and the blinding pain narrowed my vision until I could only see those two words.

I'm not a good soul. I'm a fucking thief. I could get fired or charged. Who gives a fuck anyway. I hate that job. Those people. My life. Myself. God. Who the fuck am I? What am I doing?

You're walking.

Why do I feel like I'm going to explode?

Because you are.

You're not helping.

You've gotta help yourself.

I helped myself to that cash register.

…

What? Nothing to add?

Breathe.

I'm breathing for fuck sake.

Breathe and walk.

I began stomping my feet into the sidewalk as I marched on, the melodic thud of my soles smacking against concrete made the pain ebb a bit. Desperate to dull the ache, I fingered my change pocket in search of a pill, found one, and pulled it out. Running my teeth back and forth across my tongue, trying to gather enough spit to help me swallow the pill, I wanted to bite down hard on the fleshy organ and then let the tablet ride blood into my stomach; I made fists and pressed my fingernails deep into my palms, wishing they were longer and sharper; I yearned for sharp pain, blood that could be washed away, cuts that could be bandaged, wounds that healed perceptibly.

When I tried to swallow the pill, it stopped in my throat. I gulped again and again but couldn't dislodge it. A slight burning sensation grew where the pea-sized capsule clung. It made me gag, sending hot half-digested food up into my mouth—I gulped down the hot acid and stopped walking. Standing completely still with a hand over my eyes, I willed the puke to stay down. For the pill to stay down.

"You okay, buddy?" said a male voice coming toward me.

I removed my hand from my eyes to find a hockey-jersey-wearing twenty something, with a toque that hung off the back of his head and looked like foreskin, with an exaggeratedly wide gait that kept his ill-fitting pants from falling down. He slowed his pace as he neared me.

"Yeah, I'm fine," I said, forcing a smile to wink across my face.

"All right. Take it easy," he said, speeding up and walking passed me.

I watched him hop and bounce away, his legs kicking out like those of a Ukrainian dancer's, his gait either a protest against or celebration of bipcdalism. When he glanced back at me, I turned away, tried to spit the taste of vomit from my mouth, and kept walking.

Chapter 11

"Sorry I didn't call," I said, stepping into Amy's apartment. The smell of freshly cooked food made my stomach growl, forcing a hand to my stomach to stop it from eating itself. Wading into the aroma of Amy's cooking made me realize I hadn't eaten a meal all day.

"Don't worry about it," Amy said, smiling as she shut the door behind me. "I only started cooking a bit ago."

"I mean popping in." I slipped off my shoes. "Mercy popped in on me last night, and I know how annoying it is. I wished I wasn't home."

"You're not Mercy, so I don't mind." She ran back into the kitchen and did a little pirouette on her way to the stove. "You can pop in anytime."

I sat down at her computer desk and looked at the monitor; I'd sold her that computer a year ago, with a discount. It seemed old and dated. I didn't want to look at it, and the window just behind the desk looked ripe for a computer to smash through it. Turning away from it, I took a deep breath, stood, and stepped into the kitchen, noticing that I had been biting down hard. I watched vegetables and beans fry in a pan on the stove and let my jaw relax and stretch down. It felt as if I were resting my jaw for the first time. My mouth hung open slightly but the calm I felt eclipsed the fear that I looked like a moronic mouth-breather.

"So what did Mercy want?"

"For me to watch a door."

"What?"

"Do you have any vodka?" With the alcohol out of my system, I started craving the numbness that a few drinks induces.

Amy stirred; the food in the pan sizzled and popped and made my mouth water. "Didn't you drink last night?"

"I did. I've decided to become an alcoholic."

She pulled down a bottle of vodka from above the stove and passed it to me. "When did you decide that?"

"Just now," I said, accepting the bottle from her and placing it on the counter.

Two glasses, ice cubes, an ounce of vodka, orange juice, finger stir. We clinked glasses and drank—Amy sipped, and I chugged. I made another.

"Take it easy. You'll have to stay over."

"I walked here."

She stopped stirring and turned to me; sometimes she reminded me of Mum and at that moment—with her narrowed eyes and pursed mouth, an expression that said, *I already know what you're going to say. Right now I'm both mad and disappointed. After you speak, to be fair to you, I'll voice only one of those emotions*—I could practically smell my mum's perfume.

"Where's your car?"

I looked away in response.

"Mercy has it doesn't he?" She started scraping the wooden spoon along the bottom of the pan. "You walked all the way here from work? Did he at least drop you off at work?"

"I walked there too."

Amy sighed and looked at the ceiling before turning back to me. "Why did he need your car?"

I took a sip. "His won't start."

"Of course it won't. Because he treats things like shit." Amy added something to the pan and kept stirring. "You *can* say no to him you know."

"I try. Believe me I try." I finished my drink and poured another.

Amy reached into the oven and pulled out tortillas. "It's easy. You just say, no." She kicked the oven door shut and put the tortillas on plates. "You have to treat him like a dog. Point at him and say, NO. Bad, Mercy."

It was easy for her to say, she'd always been able to say no to him and eventually he stopped asking. But he asked me all the time and, as if he held a gun to my head, yes was my only answer.

"Oh, we're having wraps. I hope that's okay."

"It smells amazing."

She lifted up the frying pan. "Plates please."

I held up the plates, and Amy spooned the delicious looking pepper, corn, bean stir-fry into the centre of the tortillas. I would have just eaten out of the pan but plates were a nice change. Then she sliced cucumber and let it fall into the tortillas. I started salivating like a dog when the cool smell of cucumber reached me. It reminded me of how Mercy, Amy, and I would run inside my parents' house on hot summer days when we were kids to find, and devour, a plate of lightly salted cucumber slices sitting in the middle of the kitchen table.

I put Amy's plate down on the counter and ate a slice of cucumber; I tasted watermelon, the other summertime snack our mum always had ready for us. The slice was delicious but the watermelon flavour made me feel drunk.

Picking up her plate, Amy said, "Where do you wanna sit? On the couch or—"

"As far away from the computer as possible," I said, eating another cucumber slice.

We sat at the kitchen table. "Work was spectacular as usual I'm guessing?" She rolled up her wrap and took a bite.

"I tried to call in sick but they wouldn't let me." I bit into the wrap, closed my eyes, and mmmed like a kid who doesn't know any better. I probably could have eaten rolled up cardboard I was so hungry but I wouldn't have traded that wrap for anything. "This is delicious by the way."

"Thanks. So why wouldn't they let you call in sick?"

"Like three other people had already called in. So I went in, sold a couple computers, and left." I took another bite and, with my mouth full, said, "Oh yeah, and Mrs. Shoemaker came in looking for a deal."

"Mrs. Poobaker? No way."

"Big way. She tried to haggle with me as if she'd just wandered off a cruise ship and into a market."

"What'd you do?"

"I told her to go somewhere else. Then she stormed out." I finished my wrap in three huge bites. Amy was still working on hers.

"No wonder you're drinking. Want another? Another wrap?"

"Both."

"Go for it."

I sat back down with more food and drink than I'd had the first time, the screwdriver a free pour, the wrap exploding at both ends.

"So what door does Mercy want you to watch for him? A bank's while he robs it?" She laughed and took a sip.

I stared at my food wondering if I should tell her, my stomach cramping at the thought of keeping it from her, turning as I pictured myself standing outside of a blood red door.

"You okay," Amy said, placing her warm hand on mine. "You're kind of white."

The food suddenly smelled too potent. I didn't want to puke, so I covered my nose with my shirt collar and breathed in the stink of my own dried sweat, making me even more lightheaded. The food felt like it was bubbling in my chest. I let the collar drop and pressed my nose into the sleeve of my shirt. I breathed in, lavender scented detergent lingered in the fibers. I exhaled, the food began to settle.

"Do you wanna lie down?" Amy said. "You're turning grey." She stood up and place her hand on my back. "Here, come to the couch."

I stood and almost vomited. "No right here," I said. "Right here." I lay down on the cool kitchen linoleum

—it made everything still. I could feel the blood coming back into my face and began to feel the cold against my back.

Amy kneeled beside me. "Are you okay?"

"Better."

"So I guess you're never coming over for dinner again."

I chuckled and so did she. "It's not the food," I said. "It's—"

"Mercy. I know. What does he want you to do? Not even selling computers makes you feel this bad."

My heart was pounding. I held it with both hands, closed my eyes, and said, "He has a friend with terminal cancer. She wants to die and asked Mercy for help." My heartbeat slowed, the nausea subsided, and suddenly I wasn't so cold. Amy just stared down at me with her mouth open. "And he asked me to help him. To 'watch his back' while he's giving her this little bottle of stuff that he's carrying around in his pocket." I sighed, feeling lighter. "I watch the door so he doesn't get caught giving her the stuff.."

Amy leaned against the table leg and started picking at her thumb again. "Holy shit. Really? I mean, he isn't just making it up is he, as some elaborate practical joke?"

"He's not that clever."

She ran all her fingers through her red hair and scratched at the base of her skull. "Are you going to do it?"

"What do you think?"

"Oh, Felix."

"What? He's going to do it anyway. And if he gets caught and I'm not there … no, it's better if I go."

"Why did she ask him?"

"I have no idea."

"What's her name? Do you know her?"

"Lisa. He's never mentioned her before."

"What about her doctor or her family, friends?"

"She asked Mercy. And that might be the most nauseating thing about it."

Amy sat up straight, grabbed her drink off the table, and downed it. "What's in the little bottle? Morphine?"

"I have no idea."

"Where'd he get it?"

I shrugged. Amy wrapped her arms around her shins, her chin resting on her knees, her eyes on me. "I guess you're just watching a door right? I mean it's her decision. She's the one doing it."

"But not without our help."

Her grey eyes were swimming with thoughts; I had to know one of them. "Would you do it? For me. I mean if I … you know, had cancer and was dying. Would you?"

"Oh, God. I don't know if I could." She shook her head. "I'd want to help you but how … how could I?"

"Picture me like Papa. Rotting in bed. Pumped full of drugs. Just getting worse and worse. Forgetting who everyone is. My room reeking of piss and shit."

"Maybe that's why Lisa asked Mercy. Because the people who love us just can't let go."

"Could you?"

"If you were …," she said, lowering her voice, "dying, and wanted help, then I'd help. But it'd be really hard."

"Why is it so much easier with animals? If they're suffering, we just do it."

"It's just harder with people. We love people more I guess."

"Or is it just a normal thing to euthanize a pet?"

Looking at Amy, at her wiggling toes, I suddenly felt hungry again. I began to sit up. Amy moved to help me but sat back when she saw that I was okay. I took my plate down off the table and began eating my second tortilla while sitting on the floor. I wanted to scooch under the table and sit there with Amy for a while.

"Your colour's back to normal, thank God. You looked like a zombie for a second there. I thought I was going to have to pull the plug."

We both chuckled. The awkwardness of a full mouth made me laugh even harder. When we'd finished, Amy said, "You hear about assisted suicide all the time, people fighting for the right to die, others getting arrested. It's legal in some places."

I slid my empty plate back onto the table, took down my glass, and chugged. "I'm just watching a door."

Amy sat up straight, her eyes and mouth gaping at me.

"What's that look for?"

"You should go there."

"Where?"

"To see Lisa," she said, shuffling forward excitedly. "To see how sick she really is so you know that you're doing the right thing. I mean, do you even know what type of cancer she has?"

"No."

"It makes sense right? All you know now is what Mercy's told you, right? So go see her for yourself. Talk to her even. Tell her who you are. Wait, can she still talk?"

"I don't know."

"You have to go. Before. You have to."

She stood up and took our dishes to the sink, pushed in the chairs and wiped the counter. I stayed seated and watched her clean the kitchen in a frenzy.

"Where is she?" she said, washing and drying her hands.

"The hospital."

"And when are you …"

"In a few days. Mercy's picking me up."

"Meet him there. Go before. Don't tell him why. God, don't tell him." Amy paced between the sink and the table. "When are visiting hours?"

"I don't know. Don't they end at five?"

"I think so. Just go before."

"What would I say to her? Hi, I'm Mercy's brother. How's the cancer?"

"If you don't go, you'll always wonder, right? I mean you're doing this to help Mercy. But you should really be doing it to help Lisa." She sat back down on the floor in front of me. "Talk to her to be sure Mercy's doing the right thing. You'll know what you want to do after you meet her."

"And what if I don't want to do it afterwards?"

"Then don't. Tell him you can't."

"And what if he gets caught?"

"He's always going to do his own thing, okay. You need to do yours," she said, more serious than I've ever seen her before. "Look at me," her tone more stern than when I was five and held a lit candle up to the tablecloth Mum had gotten as a wedding present. 'Felix, blow it out,' she had said. And I did, without thinking. When I handed her the candle, her face softened and her usual smile returned; I never wanted to see her like that again.

"After you see her," she said, "if you don't want to help Mercy, don't. If you do, do. But *don't* do it for him. He'll do what he wants whether you're there or not."

"And if he gets caught?"

"Then maybe he'll finally realize that there are consequences for the things he does."

I nodded, thinking about Mercy getting caught red handed by a nurse while he stood over Lisa's dying body.

"I guess," Amy began, sighing, "you're just watching a door, right? You're not really doing anything."

Hearing Mercy's words come out of Amy's mouth made me chuckle.

"What's funny," Amy asked, furrowing her brow.

"That's exactly what Mercy said."

We sat on the floor a while longer and we didn't speak. I had another drink. We shared a chocolate bar. Amy had class early, and I didn't want to keep her up so I got ready to leave.

"You can stay if you want."

"I should go."

"Okay. But before you go," she began, scrunching up her face as if a high-pitched sound was assaulting her ears. "I know you have a lot on your plate but could you please help me burn that program to a couple CDs? I tried to do it but it didn't work."

"Sure. How many do you need?"

"Two. No, three."

I sat down at her computer desk. "I thought only one friend needed it."

"Yeah, but then she told two friends. So …"

I went through how to do it twice, burning two discs in the process and then got Amy to burn the third disc. She bear-hugged me when she could see that the disc she had burned worked. Then she turned back to the computer and went through the process again, concentrating intently on the display in front of her. I stood, told her she didn't have to see me out, and thanked her for dinner. She wished me luck and told me to call her right after I met Lisa. I told her I'd call. She was back at it on her computer when I took a final glance around her apartment before shutting the door behind me.

On my walk home I wondered what I'd be doing twenty-four hours from that moment. How I'd feel. What I'd be thinking. Where I'd be. I wished that the whole thing with Mercy and Lisa was only a dream.

I walked and walked. When I could finally see the giant, green garbage bin spotlighted by a street light beside my apartment building, I stopped. Not ready to go inside yet—to my apartment that would remind me of Mercy, to my bed that would make tomorrow come. I picked up a rock and tossed it at the dumpster. I missed and tried again and again throwing harder and harder as if force would improve my accuracy. Then I hit it and a split second later heard the loud, hollow bang of rock on empty metal container. The extra time it took the sound to hit me was almost unnoticeable. I threw another, bigger, rock. I saw it collide with metal and then heard the aftermath as the rock had already begun to bounce off the bin. I looked behind me and saw the sound waves moving away, traveling to other more distant ears; my sounds their future and theirs, mine. Ears are living in the past. But so are eyes. Smell, taste, touch, all in the past. There is no present, only … past. And the future is past-in-waiting.

I liked the thought that Monday was already in the past, that whatever was going to happen to Lisa had already happened, that whatever I was going to decide had already been decided. That thought made stumbling into my apartment easier and collapsing on my bed bliss.

Chapter 12

That night, I had sex with Lisa.

At first, I stood in a dark, little room staring through a wall made of glass. On the other side of the glass, in an adjacent room, was a little girl's bedroom—pink flowery wallpaper, a princess bedspread, and countless stuffed animals and dolls crowding the shelves and dresser. The glass eyes of the toys stared back at me, suspicious.

Lisa lay on the bed, naked except for the hot pink nail polish on her toes. Playing with her long tawny hair and rubbing her feet together, she gazed back at me. Suddenly I was on her side of the glass wall, standing at the foot of her bed. I glanced to the room I had just been in and saw myself still standing there, staring, wearing a black suit and tie over a white button-up shirt. I turned back to Lisa. She stretched out her toes and touched my thigh—in her room, I was naked. Taking hold of her ankles, I sucked her toes, kissed her feet, and licked all the way up her soft, olive skin on my way to her lips. She pulled away when I tried to kiss her mouth. Then she was on top of me, pinning me down and inside her. She lowered her head, her hair obscuring her face and stretching down toward me. As she rocked and swayed, her hair tickled my skin like long fingers. Her eyes burned blue through the darkness of her hair; brighter and brighter and brighter they grew until I screamed and squeezed and clawed at her thighs.

I woke up, my eyelids practically too heavy to open. Throbbing beneath my boxers, I reached down to find I had soaked through them. The dream felt real, like a memory being relived, a memory I had no right to have. I wanted to give it back, to apologize to Lisa and erase it from my mind. But I couldn't. I felt as if she wanted me to have it. To have something I couldn't give back.

I blinked slowly, seeing those piercing sapphires every time my eyes closed, feeling Lisa on top of me. The weight of her, a condolence. The feel of her, a pardon.

Chapter 13

Two days later, I woke up to a phone call from Amy. She was having some computer issue and needed me right away. I didn't want to go. Mercy had my car, and it was Monday. I wanted to lie low until it was time to go to the hospital with Mercy.

"Please, Felix. It'll only take you a minute and it'll take me all day to figure out."

"Why don't we just do it over the phone?"

"It'll be easier for you to see it."

Easier for you, you mean.

"Okay. I'll be right over," I said half-heartedly.

"I'll cook you waffles to make it up to you," she sang.

I smirked and hung up.

When I smelt waffles in the hallway leading to Amy's apartment, my stomach growled, and I suddenly felt better about being there.

"Thank God you're here," she said, ushering me to the seat at her computer desk. "I'll show you what I did."

She navigated the mouse with her right hand and held her waffle-batter-covered left hand up like a surgeon about to preform an operation. "I did it like you showed me. I chose the files, clicked burn, but when I try to actually burn it," she said, clicking violently on the burn button on the screen. "Ah, see. Nothing happens." She stood up. "I don't get it because it was working fine before. I burned a bunch before and then it just froze."

"Okay," I said, taking hold of the mouse and leaning toward the glowing screen. "I'll take care of this and you take care of the waffles."

"Deal," she said, hurrying into the kitchen.

She was trying to burn the program I had gotten her, again. I wasn't sure why she needed more copies but was convinced restarting would fix the issue, so I started quitting everything that was running. When I got to her web browser, Amy's email was open. One of the subject lines popped out at me: LETTER TO SHAREHOLDER. I clicked it and started to read.

Dear Valued Shareholder,

First, I'd like to thank you, our valued shareholder, for investing in our people, our technology, our future, our startup. We enter the coming year well-positioned to take Thirsty Dragon further. We remain confident that we can deliver successful projects to our customers and that our shareholders can see another year of sustainable growth.

> I would like to thank you for your trust and support. We look forward to—

"Do you want one or two?" Amy called from the kitchen.

"Two," I said, quickly restarting the computer.

Curious where Amy got the money to invest in a company, I said, "Did you get a job?" while her computer restarted.

"What? No," she said with her back to me. "I'm just concentrating on school. I'll work in the summer."

"Any news from the Dean about that thing?" I said, swivelling from side to side in the chair.

"Actually, yeah. Her office called me this morning— ah, shit." She stuck her thumb in her mouth for a second.

"You okay?"

"Yeah. This waffle iron's hot." She plopped a waffle on a plate. "Waffles are almost ready."

"Cool. So what did they say?"

"Just to meet with them today to tell them what happened."

"Are you nervous?"

"Not really," she said, carrying two plates and waffles to the table. "It'll just be a slap on the tush."

The computer chimed, I turned back to the screen, clicked Amy's name, logged in, and tried to burn a disc —it worked.

"It's ready," she said.

I got up and sat down in front of an amazing looking waffle. The sweet smell made me start salivating. "Your disc is burning too."

"You're amazing," she said, sitting down and placing maple syrup in front of me. "How'd you do it?"

"I restarted your computer." I drenched the waffle in syrup and topped it with blueberries from the bowl that she had put in front of me. "Sometimes that's all you need to do."

"You're the best. I'll remember that for next time."

I took a bite and then another and another and another until only waffle crumbs remained on my plate. "That was amazing."

"Want another?" Amy asked with her mouth full.

"Please."

She swallowed. "There's one in the iron. It should be ready."

I burnt my fingertips taking it out of the iron and almost dropped it on the floor in my rush to get it on my plate.

"I thought you only needed three copies of that software?" I said, sitting back down.

"Yeah," she said, licking her lips slowly. "I thought so too, but word's getting around that I have it and orders keep coming in."

"How many have you given away?" I said, doctoring up my waffle for an instant replay.

She shrugged, took a bite, and said, "Fifteen."

I pulled the forkful of waffle from my mouth. "Whoa, Amy. You've gotta stop."

"Why?"

"It's one thing to pirate software for yourself but if you get caught there's a fine for each of the fifteen discs and potential jail time."

"You didn't tell me that," she said, scowling at me.

"I didn't think you'd start handing out free software like Robin Hood."

Her expression softened a bit. "What's the fine like?"

"A hundred thousand dollars I think and up to five years in jail."

"No way. That can't be right."

"Trust me. I've looked it up. People come into the store all the time wanting me to show them how to pirate stuff."

"Holy shit. But how often are people caught and prosecuted?"

"I don't know." I took a bite of waffle. "But with this plagiarism thing, if someone at the university finds out you've been giving pirated software to classmates, software required for the course, they might go after you."

Amy put down her knife and fork and stared at her plate for a moment. "What if," she said, "I'm not giving them away?"

"What do you mean?"

"What if I'm selling them?"

I put my knife and fork down. "Are you selling them?"

She nodded.

"For how much?"

"One hundred."

"So you've made fifteen hundred dollars in a couple days?"

"Yeah. Not bad for a few hours of work." She smirked.

Feeling a headache coming on, I buried my face in my hands and then pushed the heels of my palms into my eyes.

"What?"

I spoke through my hands. "Does this have anything to do with Thirsty Dragon?" I looked up at her.

Amy sat up straight. "How do you know about them?"

"You had an email open when I was restarting your computer."

"What did it say?"

I didn't respond.

"It's just a company that Josh and some other friends started up," she said.

"Didn't you used to date Josh?"

"So?"

I let it go and asked, "Where'd you get the money to invest in a startup?"

"I have money," she said, taking her plate to the kitchen.

"Fine. Do what you want. But I'd stop selling the discs and I'd get your money back from the startup.

"But in ten years I could have ten times the amount that I put in." She came back to the table and stood behind her chair, hands clasping the backrest.

"And how much would that be?"

"A hundred thousand."

"Jesus, Amy. You invested ten grand in a company called Thirsty Dragon? Where'd you get the money?"

She shrugged, looking like a guilty kid about to be sent to her room. "They are a really cool company. They're working on an app that tells you what the drink specials are around the city. So if it's Monday and you want beer, you adjust your search and can see all the beers on special everywhere."

I didn't really hear the app idea because my head began radiating pain down into my neck, so I stood, grab a glass of water, and swallowed a pill.

"Headache?" she asked.

I nodded.

"Oh," she said, covering her mouth for a moment. "Tonight's the night. I'm sorry. I totally forgot."

"That's because you were too busy using me to make money," I said, sitting down at her computer, the finished disc hanging out the side of the machine like a tongue.

"What are you doing?"

"Making sure you don't go to jail," I said, deleting the program I had downloaded for her and emptying the trash. I grabbed the disc and handed it to her. "There. Now you have one last one to sell. That should give you groceries for a couple weeks."

She took the disc, her face turning red. "Why'd you do that?"

"You're playing with fire and you don't even realize it."

"All I needed was to sell a few more."

"Why? Because you're out of money? Is that why?"

When she didn't answer, I said, "Where'd you get the money to invest in the startup?"

"My student loan. Okay?"

"Really?"

"Yeah, so what?"

"Can you even pay tuition fees now?"

"Tuition comes off the top." Her hands flew to her hips. "You'd know that if you didn't quit after high school."

I wanted to spit in her face. I could have gone to university. I chose not to. I could still go if I wanted to. And I'd work while studying. I'd pay my way not loan my way like Amy, who stood there with her hands on her hips like Mum, with a pompous look on her face like Mercy.

"At least I'm not going to get kicked out for plagiarism and violating copyright laws," I said, moving toward her door. "Maybe you and Mercy can share a cell together. Maybe they'll make an exception to the gender segregation for siblings. That'd be nice, hey."

"Don't go, okay." She stood in the middle of her apartment, looking small, lowering her hands from her hips, her expression mostly one of shame now. "I'm sorry I forgot what you had to do today. I've just been wrapped up in my own stuff."

"Why didn't you tell me you were going to sell the discs?"

"Because …"

"Because you knew I wouldn't get you the program?"

"I needed the money, okay," she said, clawing at her thumb with her fingers. "I don't have a fancy commission job like you."

I stared at her for a moment, loving and hating her simultaneously. "Thanks for breakfast," I said, before shutting the door behind me and rushing out of her building.

Chapter 14

At four o'clock in the afternoon, an hour before visiting hours were to end, the argument with Amy far from my mind, I sat in a hospital hallway, staring at the door to Lisa's room. I felt winded and couldn't move, like the time I fell backwards off the teeter-totter and landed flat on my back while Mercy, straddling the opposite end of the seesaw, cackled.

I gripped the cold, metal armrests, lowered my head, and inhaled until I thought my lungs would pop. The speckled, beige tile flooring reminded me of the halls of my high school—the tiles were identical. Holding my breath in and hoping my full lungs would lift me up and away, my mind flashed me images from my high school life: 49% in French 30, skipping gym class and smoking up in my baby vomit coloured '95 Grand Am with Mike, Mike shotgunning a can of Kokanee in three seconds, my hands up Sarah Lavender's sweater while sitting on Mike's parents' bed, Sarah's ponytail in front of me in Mr. Carpenter's Math class, the sway and flick of it bewitching. I wondered what Sarah and Mike were up to, wanted to google them, to see what they looked like almost ten years older. Mike was probably a pilot, Sarah a family doctor. *Holy fuck. The ten year reunion is next year.* Lightheaded at the realization of the impeding anniversary of a decade squandered, I exhaled, my lips flapping like the mouth of a balloon deflating as it flies around a room.

"Ten years," I said in disbelief.

The hint of a headache began scratching behind my eyes. I popped a pill, swallowed hard, and fought back nausea. I couldn't look at the floor anymore, so I turned my gaze to the doorknob in front of me— thoughts of high school vanished.

The doorknob seemed miles away as did the exit. Occasionally a nurse or a person in sickly blue scrubs pushing something on wheels walked past. I seemed to perceive these people moving down the hall just before they actually did as if I were in a constant state of déjà vu. I felt psychic and psychotic. Nothing seemed real. It seemed orchestrated for my benefit, to make me feel like I mattered. It felt as if the alignment between my physical and mental consciousnesses had blurred, like eyes crossing, double exposing the world. I knew I would stand and reach for the doorknob because I could almost see it happening, a vision of my body moving while I sat still. Going into that room was inevitable, the reason I was there, so I stood and moved forward. As I did, the worlds realigned and I could no longer perceive the future. The glitch in my brain resolved itself, and the door to Lisa's room opened before I'd reached it.

***

Half an hour earlier, I entered the hospital through a cloud of cigarette smoke made by two gown-wearing chimneys—one in a wheelchair and the other clinging to an IV stand as if it were a cane. Inside was a maze. All the hallways looked identical except for a strip of paint that ran down the centre of the halls and changed from blue to yellow to orange esoterically. I stepped up to the first reception desk I saw to get help deciphering the colour code.

"Name?" the nurse said without looking up from the computer screen that cast a cold blue glow across her face.

"Hi," I said.

The nurse raised her eyebrows before lifting her eyes to meet mine. The top half of her scrubs resembled a fun-loving Hawaiian shirt, flowers and all, while her blotchy face—too pale under her eyes, red with exertion from her bulbous cheeks down to her jowls and double chin—told the story of twenty years of hospital shift work. I didn't blame her for looking at me as if she wished I had died before stepping up to her desk because it would've meant one less thing she would have to deal with. I knew how she felt. I just wished she'd retire or go on a sabbatical or dive into the shirt she wore and lounge on a beach during the day, hula at night, and eventually swim off the fifty pounds of unhappiness that were weighing her down.

"I need to find out where someone's room is," I said, thinking the more I explained myself the more genuine I'd sound while knowing the opposite to be true. "It's my sister. She has cancer and was admitted last week. I can't remember her room number."

The lie conjured images of Amy lying in a hospital bed, alone, dying. I wanted to take it back and say something else but couldn't. I regretted berating Amy the way Dad would have, forcing her into a corner with questions I already knew the answers to, waiting for her to retaliate with a cutting comment, getting the last word—a glorious honeyed barb that poisons her— leaving her ashamed and penitent. I wanted to call her to apologize.

"She's probably up on three," the nurse said, typing on the keyboard in front of her. "Name?"

"Lisa."

"Lisa what?"

I felt my blood rush from my face, goosebumps forming on my skin, beads of sweat growing on my back—I didn't know her last name. I just nodded as if her name was Lisa What. I must have looked like one of those idiotic bobble heads.

"What's your last name?"

I pretended I didn't hear her. "What's that?" I felt like spitting in her face. I don't know why, but I could feel the saliva gathering behind my teeth.

"I need her last name, sir, so that I can find what room she's in."

"Oh." I wanted to run but instead I pulled my phone from my pocket and, putting it to my ear, I apologized to her before saying, "Hello." While I walked away pretending to talk to someone, the nurse called, "Next."

I slowly wandered away from the desk and glanced back occasionally to see if the nurse was eyeing me, but she stared at her computer screen.

I rounded a corner, put my phone away, and found an elevator. As I rode up to the third floor, the elevator rattled and hummed and felt as if the cable could snap at any moment. When the doors dinged open, I jumped off thankful to be alive. The third floor looked the same as the first, a maze with no cheese at the end. A man in scrubs walked past me; he knew where he was going, so I followed him down the hall until we hit a nurse's station and a fork; two nurses sat behind the desk, too busy to notice me. I followed the man to the right, down a hall lined with doors and empty chairs. Names were penned in black sharpie on tiny white pieces of paper beside each door. The first said FRANCIS DAUGHERTY.

I slowed to scan all the names, the hospital worker continuing on without me. Most of the doors were shut. I peeked inside the open ones—patients in gowns staggered to bathrooms, reclined or sat watching TV, or slept. At the end of the hall was an emergency exit, storage room, and a turn that ushered me to a hallway parallel to the other one and led back to the nurse's station. The hallways were identical except for a man who was hunched over in one of the chairs closest to me, his face in his hands, his back expanding and deflating with deep breaths. Walking past him, I kept scanning the name tags until, about half way down the hall, I found her: LISA P. NORRIS. Not knowing what I wanted, to run away or to step inside, I collapsed into a chair facing her door.

I stared at the door for a moment before standing and stepping toward it. When the door opened before I could reach the knob, I stumbled back and fell onto the chair—the back of my head hit the cement wall behind the chair. I grimaced and rubbed the ache for a second before letting both my hands rest in my lap. I bit down on my tongue to distract from the throb in my head.

A woman backed out of the room and closed the door behind her as if she was coming home late from a party and didn't want to wake her parents. Before she turned away from the door, I slouched and tried to look like I had just visited someone—sad and pensive instead of sweaty palmed and ready to shit myself. After the door clicked shut, she sighed, turned, and sat down beside me without looking at me. She rested her head against the wall and closed her eyes. Her shoulder-length, ash blonde hair—clearly dyed—suited her and swooped across her face, hiding her right eye. She crossed her legs, her open toe heels revealing light blue toenails that matched her fingernails. She wore a ring on the index finger of her right hand; the silver accentuated the caramel colour of her skin. As she leaned back, I wondered how the metal would taste against her skin.

She opened her eyes and began rummaging through her purse; I turned away. The purse couldn't have held more than her compact and cell phone, but she dug through it as if it were a duffle bag.

"Do you have any gum?" she said, turning to me.

"Sorry, I don't," I said, shrugging, wishing I had.

"You look familiar," she said, still rummaging through her purse. "Do you know Lisa?"

"No, I'm ah, here visiting my grandpa … he has cancer."

"Oh, I'm sorry." Zipping up her purse and letting it fall to her side, she leaned toward me. "My friend Lisa has cancer too. That's her room." She nodded to the door in front of us. "I come here almost everyday." She smiled, a sad smile, rested her head against the wall again and looked at me. Her jade eyes were made even more hypnotic by her dark eyebrows and thick eye makeup.

"How is she? Is she doin' okay?"

She shook her head and took a breath. "Your grandpa been here long?"

"About a week, but he should be coming home soon."

"That's good. Lisa's been in here a month and … well. I don't know when she'll get to go home."

I smiled and said, "Maybe sooner than you think."

"I hope so."

"I'm Felix by the way." I held out my hand.

She took my hand and with a soft shake said, "Simone. Nice to meet you."

"You too."

"How old is your friend? If you don't mind me asking."

"Same age as me … twenty-nine."

"She's really young."

"Yeah, she is." Picking at her thumbnail she said, "Your grandpa?"

"Seventy-eight."

"It must have been hard for your friend. I mean it's hard for anyone, but to get cancer so young must be really …"

"Shitty?"

"Yeah."

"She found out in grade twelve." She was looking at me but seemed to peer through mc for a moment. "It didn't seem real then. It doesn't really seem real now either. But it's been eleven years."

Her voice echoed slightly in the long hallway. I leaned toward Simone and, trying not to sound too nosey, asked, "How did she take the news when she found out?"

"I would've locked myself in my room and cried for days. Denial would've been my best friend. But Lisa." She shook her head. "I've never seen her cry. And I'm her best friend." She sniffed and wiped her nose. "You know whenever she talks to anyone about it, they always end up crying, and she ends up consoling them."

"She sounds like an amazing person."

Simone glanced at the door then turned back to me. "She didn't even cry when she first found out. Her parents bawled like little babies but not her, uh uh. I don't know what she's waiting for."

"Some people just don't cry."

"Yeah, I guess."

"It must be really hard on her parents," I said.

"It's harder on them than it is on her."

"What do you mean?"

"She's here, for them," her voice became sharp. "She never wanted any of this. To be in here, drugged up. And I can't blame her. I spent one day in the hospital when I got my tonsils out as a kid and it felt like a lifetime. The popsicles were the only thing that got me through it."

"I like the pink ones," I said.

Simone chuckled. "Purple's my favourite."

"Orange is good too."

She glanced at Lisa's door and stopped smiling. "We went wig shopping together once. After she found out. I insisted. I told her we'd get her the perfect wig so nobody'd ever know. We didn't end up buying one though. I'm sure she only went for me." She turned to me. "She never lost her hair though."

We sat in silence for a moment, the hallway as vast and quiet as an empty church. The man down the hall got up and left as we sat there. I didn't know what to say. Even though Simone didn't seem like she needed me to say anything, I wanted to tell her she was a great friend and an amazing person, that she was here for Lisa and that's all that mattered. But I had no right. I didn't know her or Lisa. So I said nothing.

"Seeing her like this makes me wonder if the treatment is worse than the disease."

When she looked at me, her eyes seemed painfully dry—no more tears for her open wound.

"But they gave her twelve more years didn't they?"

She nodded. "It felt like they were torturing her sometimes. They'd take her away and she'd come back looking half dead. But even worse than that was all the times it went into remission and came back. I probably felt a fraction of the disappointment Lisa must have felt. And now it's happening again. Same bed, different room." Simone's face drooped. "Maybe it'll go away again. Maybe it won't."

I wanted to hug her, to hold her and brush the golden hair out of her eyes.

Simone slipped off one of her shoes and massaged her heel. "You know I used to say things like, these shoes are killing me." She shook her head. "What an idiotic thing to say."

"It's just a saying. Like when people say, I'm starving, after missing a meal."

She sat up straight and appeared suddenly self-conscious. "I'm sorry," she said. "I've been talking nonstop since I sat down." Simone slid her shoe back on. "You must be sick of hearing about people you don't know. From someone you don't know."

"I like it. I'm just sick of being in this hospital."

She snickered. "Me too."

Simone licked her lips. I wanted to kiss her and find out if she tasted like strawberries or cherries. But seeing Lisa's door out of the corner of my eye made me pull away from Simone. I'd lied to her and taken things I could never give back. I was a fraud.

"How's Lisa doing today?"

She shrugged. "Okay I guess. A little spacey but okay." She pulled down gently on the bottom of her shirt. "When you leave your grandpa, do you ever think, what if this is the last time I see him? What if these are the last words I'll get to say to him?"

"Sometimes," I said, nodding. "What did you say to her today?"

"I kissed her on the forehead and said, 'Bye, Lisa Pisa.'"

"What did she say?"

"'I love you, Moe.'"

We both laughed.

"That's you? Moe?"

"Yeah. She hadn't called me that in a long time."

"So, you had a good visit with her?"

"Yeah. I could stay with her all day." She glanced at her watch. "But I wanted to leave before her parents get here. I really don't have the energy for them today." Simone rolled her eyes and shook her head. "They come everyday after work and get me to agree with them about how much better Lisa's doing. 'Look how much better she looks. Doesn't she look better? Tell her she looks better'. Ugh! It's exhausting."

She stood up and glanced down the hall; she seemed almost worried.

"Well, I should get going. It was nice talking to you." She leaned forward and touched my forearm. Her hand felt electrified. "Felix. Right?"

I smiled and nodded. "You too."

Then she let go and stood up. I wanted to stand but couldn't for some reason.

Simone adjusted her purse strap and said, "Listen, I don't have to be home for a few hours. Did you wanna go get a coffee somewhere or a shot of vodka?"

I wanted to say, *More than anything in the world*, but I felt chained to that chair. "I wish I could but … I have to stay." I immediately regretted it. She looked perfect standing there. Almost too perfect to touch.

"I understand," she said, readjusting her strap and tucking her hair behind her ears.

She looked even more beautiful with her hair off her face. Simone glanced down the hall. "Why don't you give me your number," I said, "in case I don't run into you again."

"Sure. Do you have your phone?"

I pulled out my phone and created a new blank card. She held out her hand, so I passed my phone to her. When she handed back the phone, I looked at what she'd typed before putting the phone back in my pocket.

"Thanks. I'll call you," I said, continuing, like an idiot, to just sit there. My cheeks started to burn and I hoped they weren't red. "Have a good night."

"You too."

She turned and walked away without looking back, her heel clicking on the cheap hospital floor like a steady heartbeat. I watched the sway and flick of her hair and could practically see her calves flexing beneath her jeans with each step. The hallway didn't look so lonely with her in it.

As I listened to the clicking of her heels growing more and more distant, I turned my gaze from Simone to the imposing door in front of me. I didn't know what would haunt me more, meeting Lisa and seeing what she looked like or not going in. As I tried to decide, the clicking stopped. Down the hall, a miniature Simone talked to a couple. The exchange was brief but I knew it had to be Lisa's parents. Simone disappeared but the couple got bigger and bigger with each step until their voices began bouncing off the walls and drifting toward me.

"… but why is she so pessimistic? Lisa's her best friend," said the man.

"Maybe it's because Lisa's been here for so long," the woman replied.

"She probably can't see all of the little improvements that Lisa's making everyday."

"Well, when Lisa comes home, Simone will probably cheer up."

"You're right. And she'll be home in no time. Don't let Simone's negativity discourage you, honey," he said, putting his arm around her.

She rested her head on his shoulder while they walked. "It won't." Then she had a short coughing fit, her lungs sounded tar-black and rattled deep down under the strain of a pack a day. The coughing was so loud I felt like plugged my ears. After she caught her breath and swallowed, she said, "I've already started making up her room."

The man smiled. They fell silent before opening the door into their daughter's room and slipping inside. They didn't even seem to notice me sitting there. They looked like teachers. Like regular, nice people you'd pass on the street and smile at.

What did their daughter look like? Whose eyes, nose, and mouth did she have?

If only I could have seen through their eyes when they entered Lisa's room. How would she smile, what would she say, knowing it would be the last time.

Lisa's parents were only in the room for a few minutes when the door opened and they reversed through the doorway, inching toward me.

"We'll see you tomorrow, honey, okay. Are you sure you don't need anything?" her dad said.

I leaned forward but couldn't hear the reply.

"See you tomorrow, sweetheart. Sleep well," her mum said as she kissed her hand and blew it into the room.

I couldn't see anything.

"Maybe tomorrow we can watch a movie or something," he said.

"Oh, that sounds nice."

I still heard no reply.

"Okay, goodnight, honey."

"Bye," her mum said, waving like she was leaving her child at preschool for the first time.

The door shut and Lisa's parents strolled back down the hall with their arms around each other. "She's tired. We'll come earlier tomorrow."

"She looks better today though. Doesn't she?"

"I think she's getting some of her colour back."

Watching them walk away, I felt sorry for them and I envied them. The next day, or maybe even that night, they'd get the worst news of their lives. But until then, they could wish for a healthy daughter and dream of her resting peacefully in the room they made up for her in their house.

I felt invisible, lost somewhere between asleep and awake with a calm that made me no longer feel my body. I had no heartbeat, no breath. And once again I sat alone with the door.

I stared at the name tag, tracing the letters with my eyes. LISA P. NORRIS. My eyes got stuck on the *P*. I stood up and touched it, asking it what it stood for. Then I grabbed the doorknob and twisted. I had only one question for Lisa. One question that would tell me whether to leave and never come back or to meet Mercy and go through with it—are you sure?

The door clicked open and shot forward a crack; I held the knob firm so the door wouldn't swing open on its own. My heart began to pound through my chest and head as I gripped the cold metal knob and stared at the floor inside Lisa's room. I felt lightheaded and the world began to spin and invert. I realized I wasn't breathing, took a deep breath, steadied myself, and heard the *squeak squeak* of somebody's shoes right behind me. Shutting the door, I spun around to see a nurse walk past while smiling at me pleasantly. I smiled back and turned to make my way down the hall in the opposite direction.

I don't need to meet Lisa or talk to her. She's sure. She wouldn't have asked otherwise.

Maybe she asked Mercy hoping he'd fuck it up.

No. She asked him because she knew he'd go through with it.

If you say so.

I'll stay away from Lisa. It'll be easier.

And what about Mercy?

I'll go meet him now.

"Excuse me sir," the nurse called after me.

I turned back. Afraid I had been talking out loud, my mouth hung open as I waited for her to speak.

"Visiting hours are almost over."

"Right," I said, closing my mouth and nodding. "I'm just on my way out."

She nodded. "Okay. But you still have a few minutes if you need to say goodbye," she said, before walking away.

If I need to say goodbye.

I took one step toward the exit.

Do you need to say goodbye?

Then stopped, turned, and went into Lisa's room.

The room was identical to every other hospital room I'd ever seen: everything plain, sterile, and institutional. There was a bathroom to the right of me, a TV in the far left corner, two chairs underneath the curtain-drawn window, and a little table with a box of tissue, a plastic cup, a book, and a tiny radio beside the bed. There was also a black folding chair beside the biggest thing in the room: the bed. A slight hissing sound was the only noise; I thought it was the wheeze of a radiator but as I moved closer to Lisa, I realized it was her breath, her lungs arduously pushing air in and out of her slightly open mouth. Painfully conscious of my own breathing and afraid of waking her, I held my breath and stood beside the bed looking at her. She was the girl from my dream, the playful one from the videos on Mercy's phone only paler, thinner, withered like an old woman, her lips the colour of a wilted red rose; I licked my lips as if somehow that might hydrate hers. She looked so peaceful lying there—her hair stringy and limp on the hospital gown and pillow, her arms on top of the white blankets tucked in up to her armpits— dreams her only reprieve. I looked at the IV taped to back of her hand and simultaneously wanted to pull it out and push it in deeper because it seemed to be doing nothing for her.

"I'm not asleep you know," she said, turning her head toward me and opening her eyes. "Or maybe I am. It's hard to tell these days."

I stiffened and took a step back. "I'm sorry …"

"For what?"

"I think I'm in the wrong room."

She smiled and said, "Me too."

The sides of her mouth slowly curling up put me at ease. I stared into her striking blue eyes—bright and practically glowing, they made me think of how earth looks from space, beautiful and serene. She reached for the plastic cup beside the bed, a struggle she quickly gave up.

"Would you mind?" she asked after sinking back down into the bed.

I passed the cup to her—it was full of crushed ice and looked like a slurpee with all the flavour sucked out.

She thanked me and then tilted the cup to her open mouth, tapping the back of it until ice fell forward. Lisa crunched some ice and swallowed.

"You know," she began, "If I could do it all again, I'd travel."

"Where would you go?"

"Oh, that's the question."

I sat down in the black folding chair beside her bed and looked up at her.

"Can you believe I've never been to Europe?"

"Neither have I."

Her face lit up. "Oh, you have to go. You simply must. Italy, France, Greece, Poland, Norway, Turkey." Her eyes drifted around the room as she spoke. "I'd start in Turkey I think. I've been to the States a bunch of times for tests and to see specialists. I don't know why my parents couldn't have found a specialist in Oslo. They have good doctors there too right?" She looked at me. "You really haven't been either?"

"Really."

"Where's the first place you'd—" she winced and leaned back hard into the bed, her face contorted in agony.

I sat up straight and moved to the edge of my chair. "Should I get someone?"

She held up her non-IV hand, it ticked in the air like the broken second hand of a clock that never moves forward, her face relaxing.

"It's okay. They come and go." She breathed deeply for a moment with her eyes still closed. Then she turned to me, opened her eyes, and said, "Where's the first place you would go?"

"I don't know," I said, leaning back in the chair. "I've ... I've never really thought about it."

"What if you had a year left to live? What would you do? Where would you go?"

"I'd quit my job. I know that."

"And then what?"

Her voice was soothing, like in the videos but softer.

"I don't know. Maybe I'd travel. Fall in love. Watch the sunset on every continent. Walk naked on a beach. Ride in a helicopter. Laugh. I'd want to laugh as much as possible."

"Um, I haven't had a good hard laugh in a while."

"Me neither."

She gazed at me, her slow-moving eyelids hypnotic. "That all sounds pretty good. Maybe I'll get to travel there after I die. Maybe there's a moment right before death when a person can go anywhere and see anything and be there as long as they want."

"Maybe you can go when you get better."

"There's no getting better. Not this time."

Not wanting to look into her eyes at that moment, I looked down at the floor.

"But it's okay. I'm not afraid. Just disappointed that I didn't get to travel," she said. "Have you thought of where you'd go yet?"

"Turkey sounds nice. I don't know anything about it though."

"One thing I've heard is that there are cats everywhere."

"Really? Why?"

"I don't know. I guess they just love cats and they let them roam around the city like cows in India. Apparently even Hagia Sophia smells like cat piss."

"What's Hagia Sophia?"

"Oh, it's this amazing, super old building in Istanbul that was a basilica and then a mosque and now a museum."

"But it smells like cat piss?"

"I guess so. I read a blog post from this guy who was there, and he said it smelt like old hiking boats and cat piss."

"That sounds like the absolute worst combination of smells."

"How about rotten eggs rubbed on a fat man who hasn't showered in a year?" she said.

"Oh." At the thought, my hand flew to my nose instinctively. Then I began to chuckle.

"There's always something worse."

"I don't even want to know what's worse than that," I said.

"How about—" she began, a mischievous smile creeping across her face.

"Please stop," I said, laughing out loud."

"Okay," she said, the mischief leaving her smile. "I'd still love to smell it though. Hagia Sophia I mean. Not rotten eggs and unwashed people."

"Well, I can leave a filthy litter box and my ten-year-old hiking boots in the corner of your room and let the potpourri of Turkey massage your nose."

Now she chuckled. "That's really sweet of you."

Looking at each other, our smiles faded. Lisa was never going to see anything outside of that hospital room again, and we both knew it.

"Well," I said, "if you get to have that moment when … you know, go there first."

"I will and then I'll visit you to tell you about it."

"Thanks."

"When you smile," she said, "you remind me of someone."

"Really?"

"Yeah. Someone who's supposed to visit me tonight."

"Aren't visiting hours over?"

She shrugged. "You're here aren't you."

"But I'm not supposed to be."

"I think you are."

We sat in silence for a moment, looking at each other, the IV on her hand more conspicuous somehow. I wanted to pull it out and carry her to the airport.

"I'd take you to Turkey if I could."

Slow blink, slow blink. "I know." Slow blink, slow blink. "Maybe in another life."

I heard the *squeak squeak* of shoes hurry down the hall past Lisa's door.

"I should go."

Lisa watched me stand, saying nothing.

I wanted to hug her, to kiss her cheek, to squeeze her hand, anything. But all I could do was smile and wave.

As I walked toward the door, she said, "See you in my dreams."

I turned and said, "See you in mine."

She waved with her IV hand, and I left.

The door latching behind me seemed to echo in my ears as I moved down the hall. Putting one foot in front of the other, feeling untethered from gravity, my feet sticking to the ground felt like a conscious choice rather than an inescapable law.

Chapter 15

While making my way out of the hospital, I ended up in the packed emergency waiting area. One guy had a bloody towel pressed against his eye. A woman, who looked dead, lay sprawled across the floor while a male and female paramedic, wearing matching blue latex gloves and uniforms, stood looking down at her. I tried not to stare while making my way outside. Stepping through a gang of smokers trying to hotbox the entranceway, I made my way to some nearby grass and sat down to wait for Mercy. I had called him that morning to tell him to meet me outside emergency. He liked that plan better because it meant he didn't have to pick me up in *my* car.

As I sat waiting for him, I watched the smokers. They looked like withered versions of the cool high schoolers I used to see smoking during spares and lunch breaks everyday in Grade Twelve. A shrivelled old lady leaned desperately against the wall and appeared propped up by the brick; I couldn't tell if she was sucking the life out of the cigarette or if it was the other way around. A vision of me shoving the cigarette down the old lady's throat infected my imagination. Seeing my hand covering her mouth, her bulging eyes, made me shake my head in an attempt to dislodge the fantasy, but it stayed until I lay down and looked at the sun—the heat and glare of it whitewashed my sight and mind.

For a moment, there was nothing, a quiet intent to get through the night with only my breath to accompany it. Then my mind started to scream—*I heard Mercy laughing, saw Lisa smiling, the nurses' scowls, the shrivelled smoking lady spitting, my mum sitting in her TV chair staring at me, Lisa's parents hugging, Dan yelling, "Sell," Simone's lips, computers, customers, customers, every customer I'd ever helped, Amy's hug, smile, and eyes, computer screens, Lisa's IV hand, doctors scribbling on clipboards, hospital hallways, Lisa's door, the knob, my bed, her bed, my car, needles, the little bottle filled with death, Mercy's face, Lisa's naked body morphing from supple and seductive to sickly and repulsive and back again, pain ... nothing, sweet nothing ... Mercy's fist, the moon, traffic, was it real, was I real, what's the point, does it matter? Does anything matter?*

A hand squeezed my shoulder; it was real; I was real. It squeezed and everything disappeared but the touch on my skin and the electricity. My eyes sprung open and shot to the hand—its veins pulsing overtop of the strong grip; its light brown hair, delicate and soft.

"Hey, buddy," Mercy said.

I looked up at him. He was upside down, squatting beside me. "Hey," I said, smiling, feeling suddenly calm. I saw my own eyes staring back at me. I hadn't notice that our eyes were an identical blue grey until that moment.

"Why are you lyin' on the ground? There's chairs over there?"

"I'm just enjoying the grass."

He stood. I sat up.

"You ready?" he said, standing behind me.

I glanced at the old lady still smoking and nodded.

"Let's go."

He marched toward the hospital. I stood and followed.

"Isn't it a little early?"

"Not to eat," he said, turning to me and grinning, tapping my stomach with the back of his hand.

I was craving something too, but couldn't eat. Water was all I wanted. I followed one step behind him as we went inside and entered the cafeteria. The smell of hospital food made me loath the idea of eating. The calm I'd felt outside on the grass turned into an alertness that bordered on paranoia.

"I ate here yesterday," he said. "They have these great half chickens." He licked his lips. "Last night, it got a little cold before I finished, so I got "em to nuke it in the microwave for a bit to warm it up, and it was even better."

He acted liked he'd discovered ambrosia, but I was pretty sure that nuked hospital food wouldn't make anyone immortal.

"You want anything?"

I shook my head, no, and sat down at one of the empty tables. Mercy walked away whistling. He acted as if we were going to a movie or something. My phone began vibrating as I watched him saunter away—it was Amy. I didn't answer and turned off my phone; I wasn't going to need it for a while.

A bunch of people, most in scrubs, sat in the cafeteria. I watched their jaws bouncing up and down, their eyes fixed on phones held by non-fork holding hands. Just another shift for them.

The cafeteria was plain, everything painted an institutional green. Just sitting there made me feel ill and in need of hospitalization. Mercy returned and placed a plastic tray on the table before sitting down across from me, the chicken carcass steaming, a can of coke beside it. The bird looked radioactive and was hot enough to cause the styrofoam plate beneath it to melt and curl up. I wanted to laugh at the lemon wedge and parsley garnishing the side of the plate.

Mercy looked up at me before digging in. "You want some?"

"No thanks."

He started shovelling it in like a caveman who hadn't eaten in days. "Oh, this is good." I could see the chewed up flesh as he spoke. He picked up the parsley and shoved it in his already full, greasy mouth and then squeezed the lemon onto the ripped up half a bird. It made me think of squeezing lemon on an open sore; I cringed at the thought.

He ripped and pulled and sucked the bones dry. He was a vulture picking it clean. When he finished stuffing his face—and I never wanted to eat again—he wiped his glistening mouth and hands on a paper napkin and downed the can of coke. As he picked at his teeth with a finger and tongued the bits of meat stuck between his teeth, he said, "That was good."

"How can you eat?"

"What?"

I glanced around and leaned forward. "With what we're about to do, I just can't believe you're even hungry."

"Why? I have to eat." He wiped his mouth with the back of his hand. "I haven't eaten enough protein today. You know—" he belched "—you're supposed to eat your weight in protein everyday."

I leaned back. "That's impossible. Nobody could eat their body weight in protein in a week let alone twenty-four hours."

"In grams. Your weight in grams of protein. So I should be eating 220 grams of protein a day."

"Where'd you hear that?"

"Read it in a magazine."

No doubt one that featured a baby-oiled man, with a neck bigger than my thigh, carrying a ripped, bikini-wearing woman on his steroidal shoulders on the cover.

"Don't believe everything you read."

"It's true. I heard it somewhere else too."

He probably read it twice in the same magazine or heard it from a friend who had read the same article.

"Do you have everything?"

"Yep!" he said lifting his tray and preparing to stand.

His greasy fingerprints were all over his side of the table. I grabbed the last unused napkin from his tray, reached over, and began wiping the table clean, my hand shaking.

Mercy saw my tremor. "What's up?"

"Are you really going through with this?"

"I promised her I would."

"God, this is crazy."

"It's crazy not to do it."

I leaned back in the uncomfortable cafeteria chair and took a deep breath. "How are you so calm?"

I'd never felt more unsure in my life, but Mercy seemed more at ease than ever.

"Don't worry. It'll be fine." He looked at his watch while licking his lips. "We should go."

He got up, placing the tray back down on the table and leaving it there. I followed, trailing a few steps behind with the tray. He didn't wait for me while I slid the bird remains into the cafeteria garbage, stacked the tray on a pile, and recycled the empty pop can; I had to hurry after him.

Why am I here? How did Mercy talk me into this?

You're here for Lisa. And you talked yourself into it.

That's bullshit.

You're bullshit.

Mercy pushed the elevator button, and I caught up to him. As we stood there waiting for the metal doors to open, not saying anything, I felt nine years old again.

Me and Mercy were standing on the beach looking at a motionless crab.

"Throw a rock at it. See if it's alive," he said, pushing me forward.

"No! You!" I shrugged his hand off my back.

He kicked some sand at the crab but it didn't move.

"Hey. I'll piss on it and see if it moves."

Mercy pulled down the front of his swimsuit, pinched the end of his penis, and stepped forward, leaving small footprints in the sand as he approached the crab with his weapon drawn. When he stood within range directly in front of it—the crab trapped between Mercy's feet and the wall of rocks behind it—he said, "Watch to see if it moves."

The warm, yellow stream hit the shell and splashed everywhere, making the crab and rocks glisten while the sand absorbed the moisture. Mercy laughed and pinched short bursts onto the crab's shell. I ran forward pulling down my trunks. Our piss bounced off and shot back at our bare feet—we jumped back cackling and pushing out our last drips.

"I think it's dead," Mercy said, shaking himself.

The rocks, crab, and sand started to dry in the sun.

"Throw a rock at it."

"You!"

"C'mon. It's dead anyway. Just throw one."

"Fine."

The closest rock was one the size of my hand. I picked it up and tossed it. The rock hit the crab right in the centre of its shell, cracking it wide open. The crab jerked into a frenzy of sideways movements and slow-motion clawing. It reached up to its split shell, its mouth flapping like a fish out of water. It looked like a windup toy set on berserk. It tried to scale the steep rocks behind it but kept slipping and falling back down.

With my mouth wide open and my feet buried in hot sand, I stood frozen. Mercy ran over and picked up a rock that was bigger than the crab.

"It's suffering. We have to help it," he said, raising the huge rock over his head.

Mercy brought the rock down, his arms swinging with the force of a sledgehammer. The loud crunch splashed blue goo onto Mercy's feet and made me throw up all over my bare chest. The crab's legs tensed beneath the rock. We watched the crab twitch, its convulsions a protest against its own death. I wished back my throw and stared until the crab stopped moving.

The elevator doors dinged open and we stepped inside. It was hot like the beach in that elevator; I could almost feel the sand between my toes and the weight of a rock in my hand. As we neared the third floor, I looked over at Mercy—all I could see was a little boy holding a gigantic rock over his head.

Chapter 16

We exited the elevator, walked past the vacant nurse's station and down the hallway before sitting in the chairs facing Lisa's door. I sat in the same chair as before; the cushion felt stuffed with tacks—I couldn't sit still.

Mercy checked his watch. It was almost 7:45, and we were in a ghost town. He glanced down the hall. "I should go in." He stood up and looked down at me. "Watch the door and make sure nobody comes in. No matter what."

I didn't say anything. I didn't even move. He stepped forward and grabbed the doorknob. Putting his free hand in his pocket—no doubt gripping the little bottle of liquid death—he smiled into the room before disappearing. The door latched, and it was 5 o'clock again; I was all alone, trying to persuade myself to go into Lisa's room; Mercy hadn't just gone into her room; he wasn't even there yet; and I still had plenty of time to figure things out. I expected Simone to exit Lisa's room at any moment and I refused to check the real time.

Standing up, my knees wobbled; I had to steady myself by placing a hand on the cold, brick wall. When my knees regained their strength, I began to pace up and down the hall, passing the door each time and staring at it.

Has he given it to her yet?

Are they talking?

What is he saying?

What is she saying?

Has he given it to her yet?

I stopped pacing and pressed my ear against the door—nothing, just the sounds of my ear squishing into cold metal.

What's taking him so long? He just needs to give her the bottle and leave.

I thought I heard them talking inside the room; straining to hear, I held my loud breath for a few seconds, trying, in vain, to decipher the muffled voices.

Mercy might be the last person she ever sees.

That's fucked up.

Well, that's what she wants. It's her life.

I didn't realized I was flexing my entire body, as if trying to hold back diarrhea, until my jaw and fists started to ache. Gasping in a frantic breath, I relaxed and managed to avoid shitting myself.

I wouldn't want Mercy to be the last person I'd ever see.

Then who?

Amy.

No really. Who?

I told you. Amy.

Come on. Who?

Fuck off.

Who?

You know who.

Why can't you say it.

I can say it.

Can you? … Who?

Me, okay. I'd want to see me. I'm a narcissistic asshole. Happy? Me, me, me. An out of body experience or my doppelgänger would be perfect. No one else.

I imagined Mercy handing over the bottle—Lisa drinking it, filling a syringe with it before stabbing a vein and plunging.

It was done. I could sense it. Sighing and feeling as if I'd just run a marathon, I smiled and chuckled a little. Lisa's pain was gone, years of pain, of feeling like her life wasn't her own, gone. She'd snatched her life from those who had claimed it, held it close before letting it go. And Mercy had helped, had been the instrument, had done the right thing.

I'll kill myself if I'm ever dying slowly, painfully. And if I need help, I'll ask … who will I ask?

You know who to ask.

I'll ask Mercy. I'll fucking ask Mercy. He did it for Lisa. He'd do it for me.

I stepped back away from the door wanting to switch places with Lisa, to be the one holding Mercy's hand, our hands complicit, sealing a pact. I imagined her hand in his as life drained out and made it limp. Then his hand became mine, and I stood squeezing Lisa's lifeless hand, leaning down and kissing it before letting go.

It should have been me in that room. I could have done it. Why the fuck would she trust Mercy and not me?

She doesn't know you.

She does too. Her eyes looked through me. She knows me.

I wanted to punch the brick wall, to shatter every bone in my hand and watch the blood trickle down white brick before dripping onto the cheap tile floor, but the masochistic urge vanished when I heard footsteps coming toward me. The sound, like handcuffs tightening round my wrists, made me cringe. Trying not to look suspicious, I turned slowly. I felt grotesque, as out of place as a person streaking the halls of a funeral home. The footsteps belonged to a heavyset nurse with a dyke haircut, who marched straight for me —she had something in her hand, something for Lisa. I had to keep her out of the room. I eyed a chair and considered throwing it at her and then stuffing her unconscious body into a storage room.

When the nurse got closer, I leaned, with my hands in my pockets, against the wall beside the door. She veered toward me.

"Visiting hours are over," she snapped, stopping in front of me, her voice like shards of glass flying into my ears. "You have to leave."

"I know, but I'm here with my brother. He forgot something in his friend's room when he was visiting him today."

"What's his friend name?"

"Francis Daugherty." The name had flashed in my mind and flew out my mouth instinctually. It was the first name I had read in the adjacent hall.

The nurse glanced at Lisa's name written on the tag beside the door. "Where's his room?"

"Just down the hall. I was wandering around."

"Well, you have to leave once your brother collects his belongings. Okay?"

"Of course. Two minutes."

Waiting for her to take the first step, not knowing what I'd do if she reached for the doorknob, I tried to get a look at what she held in her hand but couldn't tell what it was. I forced myself to smile. She smirked back and stepped down the hall away from the door. I sauntered away from Lisa's room, listening to the nurse's footsteps. When her shoes stopped clicking, a door opened. I spun around to see the nurse vanish into a room at the end of the hall. Hoping it was a stairwell to take her to another floor, I knew she'd be back in five minutes to make sure I was gone, so I marched back to Lisa's door and almost went in, but I couldn't interrupt them.

I glanced at my phone—7:55pm. "Please come out. Please come out. Please come out," I whispered at the door. And he did. Me and Mercy almost knocked heads when he emerged because I stood so close to the door. His smile was gone and sweat glistened all over his pallid face.

"What happened?"

Shaky and looking like he was about to faint, Mercy kind of leaned against me to steady himself. I shuffled backward from the weight of him and then helped him to the chairs where he collapsed.

I sat beside him. "You okay? 'Cause we don't have a lot of time. A nurse is gonna be back here in like two minutes." I stood up, ready to leave. "Let's go."

"You don't get it."

"Well, you can help me get it once we're outta here."

"No. I couldn't do it."

"What? Why not? What happened?"

He stared at the door. "She was just lying there sleeping. Her eyes moving under her eyelids. I … I watched her the whole time. I couldn't wake her up." He shook his head. "I couldn't wake her up."

"What do you mean you couldn't wake her up? You promised her. What happened? She's waiting for this. She's waiting for you."

"I know, but I can't. I thought I could, but I can't."

"But she's ready. She needs this today."

I wanted to smack him out of whatever daze he was in. Mercy hunched over in the chair, arms pressed against legs, the little glass bottle teetering in his right hand.

"You have to go back in there."

"I know. But I can't." He looked up at me and held out the bottle. "Here. You do it. Take it."

I threw my hands up in the air. "No no no no no. She asked you. This is your thing. This is between you and Lisa."

He stood and staggered toward me like a drunk, his eyes were wild and wide with panic. "Just, just tell her I sent you. Just tell her I said it was okay." He pushed the bottle into my hand; it was warm and moist with sweat.

I tried to push it back but he put his hands behind his back. "God damn it, Mercy. You were supposed to do this. Lisa is counting on you to do this."

"You have to do it."

I looked down at the label—U-500 - REGULAR HUMAN INSULIN INJECTION.

"What the hell is this? Insulin?"

He reached into his pockets and then thrust a thin plastic syringe and a t-shaped thing with a purple plunger into my hands. "Empty the bottle of insulin into the needle and put it in her shoulder."

"What's insulin gonna do? Regulate her fuckin' blood sugar?"

"It's enough to kill her."

I glanced down at the tiny bottle; it suddenly had the weight of a gun.

"What's this other thing for?"

"It's a pain killer. After the insulin, spray that under her tongue a couple of times and you're done."

I glanced down the hall at the door the nurse had disappeared behind, hoping she'd emerge to kick us out but also that she'd fallen down the stairs and lay unconscious. I turned to face Mercy. He looked as if he were about to puke, faint, or both.

"Please, Felix," he said. "Please."

"Fine. How much of the insulin?"

"All of it."

I stared at the drugs in my hands and said, "I can't believe I'm doing this. You better watch this door like your life depends on it." I grabbed the doorknob and twisted. "If anyone comes in, I'm jumping out the fucking window."

The next thing I knew, I was in Lisa's room, again standing at her bedside.

I reached out to grab her hand but pulled back. I opened my mouth to wake her but couldn't find the words. Unable to hold my breath any longer, I gasped and started to pant. Breathing harder and harder, I looked at the bottle in my shaking hand, took one last look at Lisa, and turned to leave. I couldn't do it either. I reached for the door but one word stopped me, "Please." Lisa's voice, an angelic whisper, made me turn back. "Please wait."

I turned to find her propped on her elbows watching me. I returned to her bedside, her eyes were an ocean blue fixed on me.

"I can't," I said.

"Please. Please. You have to. It's why you're here."

Lisa adjusted her pillows and sat up further. She was surprisingly agile. Then she reached out and took my hand, her unexpected warmth went through my entire body. I looked down at our interlaced fingers, then back into her eyes. A tear streamed down my cheek and hit the bed.

She squeezed my hand. "It's okay. It's what I want. Help me." I let go of her hand and wiped my eyes. I couldn't remember the last time I had cried, and it didn't matter.

She grabbed my wrist, her delicate touch holding me as I placed the pain killer sprayer on the bed, removed the cap from the syringe, and emptied the bottle of insulin into it. With her free hand, Lisa pulled her sickly blue hospital smock down to expose her shoulder and then gathered some flesh between her fingers.

As I raised the syringe and slid the empty insulin bottle into my pocket, she said, "Not too deep."

I squeezed her arm with my free hand, her hand gripping mine tighter, and let the needle hover above her flesh.

"Do it," she said.

Without looking at her, I moved my hand forward and the tip of the syringe vanished into her skin. My thumb pressed down until it couldn't anymore. I jerked back my hand—a drop of blood appeared and began to grow where the hole was. Lisa let go of me and dabbed the blood with a tissue. She then covered her shoulder and held out the tube of pain killer to me.

"Now this," she said.

I put the cap back on the syringe and dropped it into the disposal unit mounted on the wall that read BIOHAZARD - AUTHORIZED PERSONNEL ONLY across the top.

I took the t-shaped thing from Lisa and locked my fingers around it as if it were a syringe, my thumb poised on the purple plunger. Lisa watched me the whole time and let her mouth fall open. I positioned the spout in her mouth and squeezed, once, twice, three times before pulling away. Squeezing my arm, she closed her eyes and swallowed.

"Again," she said, her eyes still closed.

"What?"

She opened her eyes. "Do it again."

I put the device in her mouth again. Lisa gently slid her hand to my wrist, staring at me. Again I squeezed three times, holding my trembling hand up until she let go of my wrist. Lisa lay back, her entire body sinking deeper into the bed, her hand falling down to the sheets. She closed her eyes and tears danced down her cheeks before soaking into the pillow. Then she opened her eyes, smirked, and took my hand in hers. I glanced back at the door and then looked at her.

"Thank you," she said, squeezing my hand before letting go. "I told you you weren't in the wrong room."

I bowed and turned to leave. At the door I turned back; Lisa blew me a kiss. I instantly thought of the video of her blowing a kiss to the camera on Mercy's phone, and for a moment she appeared just as she had in the video, colour rushed back to her face, her lips became a full and deep red; she looked young, happy, alive. I waved and left, shoving the pain killer into my pocket.

The door latched behind me, and I leaned against it in the hallway facing Mercy. He didn't notice me at first because he had his elbows on his knees and his face in his hands. I wiped my eyes, took out my phone, and turned it on—8:22pm.

"We should go," I said.

Mercy's head shot up. He jumped to his feet, colour back in his face.

"What happened? Did you do it?"

I nodded. Mercy looked at me intently, smiling, nodding, his smile growing as he nodded. I turned and started down the hall. He followed my lead and wrapped his arm around my neck.

"Nicely done, buddy."

As we walked to the elevators, Mercy's arm tightly around me, practically holding me in a headlock.

"How'd it go? Did you give her everything? Was she okay with you there? Did she ask about me? Did she ask who you were? Was it okay? Of course it was. Did you say who you were? Did you tell her you were my little brother?"

I pretended not to hear him. At the elevators, I pushed the down arrow. I kept picturing Lisa in her bed, asleep with a smile on her face, slowly losing consciousness for the last time.

The hospital seemed deserted. Mercy kept flexing his arm around my neck and staring at me.

"Good job, buddy. Good job. We did it. We did it."

As his words left his mouth, I wanted to shove them down his throat and break the arm that felt like fire on my skin. He hadn't done anything. He never did anything. And he forced me to do what he couldn't. I pushed him off as hard as I could and rubbed my skin where his arm had been, trying to wipe away his touch.

He stumbled back. "What's up with you?"

"You have no idea what just happened, do you?"

"I ah—"

"Shut up! You don't know anything. This isn't a game. It's not fun."

"I never … I don't …"

"You don't know anything about anything. You don't even know how to play hockey. You know how to fight. But that's it. You ever score a goal, Murse? Huh? Or were you too busy dropping your gloves." I leaned in and wanted to hit him. "You're just a selfish idiot who lives with his parents."

Mercy stood still for a moment. Then he stepped forward, and I shoved him with both hands. As I leaned into his chest, his fist connected with the side of my jaw. I hit the elevator door and dropped to my knees, dizzy, my ears ringing, my jaw exploding with pain.

"Sorry, Felix," he said with his palms up, backing away.

My jaw felt dislocated. I held it and got up. "I deserve that sorry."

The elevator doors dinged open. I turned away from my brother and tossed open the stairwell door without looking back.

Chapter 17

A big metal door stood guard at the bottom of the stairs; I kicked it open and stumbled into the glow of streetlights and the still night air. I was alone on an abandoned side of the hospital. The silence was infuriating. I turned to go back inside but the door, which had no handle, had latched. I kicked the door again and again, the sound of denting metal echoing before then being swallowed by the night. I kicked and screamed until my throat burned and my foot ached. When all the air spilled out of my lungs, I gasped and stumbled onto the grass where my knees gave out and I collapsed. On my back, I stared up at the sky trying to catch my breath. The moon shone blood red and blanketed the world in a crimson glow. I reached up to touch it, but the red disappeared behind the weight of my eyelids.

I woke up to the sounds of sniffing. A rabbit, with a mouthful of grass, sniffed my face and hopped away. I sat up feeling drunk but alert, like a knocked-out boxer after a whiff of ammonia. When I managed to get to my feet, the rabbit bolted and then stopped a few metres away with his ears erect. I tried to tell him I wasn't going to hurt him but my jaw throbbed and stopped the words from forming.

The moon was higher in the sky now and no longer red. While stumbling away from the grass matted in the shape of my body, I wondered if I had imagined the red glow cast upon the world when I passed out.

It was 10:30pm. I looked at the hospital and wished I could see through walls and up into Lisa's room, to see if she was still breathing. Not knowing for sure if she were alive or dead made me feel like biting red ants crawled all over me. I stepped up to the door I had dented. Without a knob or handle, I would've needed a crowbar to open it, so I ran around the building until I spotted a door that opened. Inside, I found stairs and ran to the third floor. Sweating and panting, I burst out of the stairwell searching for Lisa. The elevators were in front of me, so I sprinted in the direction of Lisa's room and flew past the still vacant nurse's station. I stopped and ducked behind a corner when I saw a nurse reaching out for Lisa's door. The door opened and closed behind her. Hunched over, holding my knees and wheezing, I waited for the nurse to scream or call out for help or for other nurses and doctors to run past me toward Lisa's room. Eager to hear something, I quieted my breath, but the hall remained silent and no one came running. I looked down the hall a moment later; the nurse exited the room and entered another.

It was done and nobody knew. Lisa would die sometime during the night, nobody to hold her hand and tell her they loved her. Nobody to kiss her forehead and tell her it was okay. I stared down the hall wanting to see her one more time, wanting to be there with her, for her, until the end. Lisa didn't want me there though. She didn't need to be comforted. I had done what she needed me to do and now she needed to be alone. I left the way I came, sauntering down the halls and stairs, feeling eerily calm. When my phone rang and I saw it was Mercy, I ignored the call and put the phone back in my pocket.

Lisa was probably dying while I walked through the parking lot next to Emergency. I weaved between cars, picturing her gasp for breath. I rapped my knuckles on lampposts imagining her chest convulse. I kicked the stupid yellow lines painted on the concrete, imagining the pulse in her neck slow and then stop.

Everything became still. The world was muted. Not even the soles of my shoes on gravel made a sound. An ambulance leisurely drove down the road toward Emergency, no siren just flashing lights. I saw my car, abandoned at the end of the parking lot. The door made no sound when I opened and closed it behind me. The keys were in the ignition; they dangled back and forth as if Mercy had just put them in the ignition and left. When I turned the key, the engine roared, sirens howled, and the song on the radio blasted my ears. I shut off the radio and started to drive.

On my way home, I felt as if I hadn't slept for days. My movements were slow and deliberate. My head and body swayed with the ebb of the tires on the road. I could have been floating in outer space, the lights of the city streaking by like falling stars. I made it to my apartment, like a programmed robot. When I collapsed in my bed, I actually heard my eyelids shut.

I heard them open again at ten in the morning the next day when I woke up fully dressed. The sun almost blinded me it was so bright. I didn't want to move for at least a week and that's when the phone rang. While listening to the ringing, thinking it was probably Mercy, I realized I should have been at work at nine.

I sat up and grabbed the phone. "Hello," I rasped with a certain ghastly quality that made me sound like I was calling from purgatory.

"Oh my God. You're not still in bed are you?" Kurt said.

"Ah, yeah. I ah, forgot." My jaw hurt when I spoke, so I placed a hand on it and wondered how bad the damage was.

"You forgot? I don't know how you could just forget that you have to work, Felix. I'm beginning to think you're not a team player anymore." He paused, breathing into the phone. "Well, are you a team player, Felix?"

"Listen I just forgot, okay."

"Well, that doesn't sound like the kind of thing a team player would do now does it?"

I wasn't in the mood to play his stupid games. At first I felt bad but then I just wanted to hang up on him. "I feel awful, and I can't make it to work today."

"Really? And you're telling me this an hour after you were supposed to be here? Have you forgotten about giving us a little notice if you can't come in? Calling the night before? Or at least a few hours before your shift?"

"No, I just—"

"Forgot. Right. Well, you'll have to find somebody to take your shift if you can't come in."

"Are you serious?"

"Do you have any reason to think I'm not serious?"

"But I don't have anyone's number."

"Whose do you want?"

I could hear pages being flipped.

"I've got all the numbers right in front of me."

I wanted to reach through the phone and smack him. As if one less salesperson would have made any difference to the fifty wandering around the store. And it was Tuesday, only a fraction busier than Monday, the deadest day of the week. I'd probably sell two printers in eight hours and not even make enough to pay for gas. The thought of selling people crap all day made me wanna puke, especially when I couldn't even sell myself a reason to get out of bed. Just the thought of stepping into that building made my stomach turn.

"I'm not calling anyone," I said.

"What?"

"You heard me."

"No, I don't think I did."

"Yeah, well, don't expect me today, tomorrow, or any other day. Okay. I'm done."

"Maybe you wanna think this over."

"Maybe *you* should think this over."

"What's that supposed to mean?"

"I'd explain it but I don't think you'd understand anything without a dollar sign in front of it."

"I see how it is. Suddenly you're too good to work here. You've been acting high and mighty for a while now but you listen to me—"

"No, I don't think I will." Then I hung up. And it felt good, the right choice without regrets. The only thing better would have been seeing the expression on his face as I did it.

The phone rang again and again and it just kept ringing, but I didn't answer it. At first I thought it was Kurt and then I thought it was Mercy and then I briefly thought that it was the police calling to question me about being in the hospital the night before. I wouldn't look at it, and it finally stopped ringing.

I lay back down, curious about what would happen to Lisa's body. Her parents would probably have an open-casket funeral. I wondered how they would dress her and how they'd do her hair and makeup?

They'd try to make her look as alive as possible for everyone who came to see her. The mourners would say, *She was so young. So beautiful. It's not fair.* She'd be an ornament of herself, one of those little glass collectables that people put in their hutches. After they saw her and gave condolences, would everyone eat and drink and socialize as if it were a wedding? Would anyone talk about the hockey scores, how well their team is doing, their cool new phone, or something funny they'd seen on the internet, a movie, or TV show they'd just watched? Would anyone complain about how bad the food was? Or how boring the service was?

I'd hate it if my funeral was like that, but Lisa wouldn't mind. If it would've made her parents happy, it would've been fine with her. Buried in the ground in a box with a trite epitaph ("Beloved Daughter," "An Angel Taken Too Soon," "She Fought an Uphill Battle and Won") didn't seem right even though it had nothing to do with her.

Ashes scattered on a calm day in the middle of the ocean or in a forest by a stream, that's how I pictured her final resting place and that's how I'd remember it no matter how it was going to happen because I wouldn't be there; I could imagine whatever I wanted.

The phone kept ringing and somehow, as if it were a lullaby sung just for me, I fell asleep.

Chapter 18

Lisa was waiting for me. She took my hand and pranced beside me, almost dancing in her white dress, her flaxen hair playing in the breeze, her radiant skin kissed by the sun. She led me down an empty downtown street. The only other people around were staring down at us from the windows of huge sky-scrapers; hundreds of faces watched us as we strolled down the barren street. Barefoot and avoiding the huge cracks in the road, I could feel the jagged concrete digging into my feet, the frozen road making my soles ache with frostbite. We moved as one down the centre of the road—Lisa on one side of the solid yellow line and me on the other. Our hands and interlaced fingers hung directly over the line between us. Lisa didn't seem to notice the countless faces staring down at us, but my eyes kept drifting up toward their hot gaze that would have seared my flesh had I let go of Lisa's hand. She kept pulling my arm to force my gaze from the buildings to the path before us. We followed the road out of the skyscraper jungle into the sun, which was no longer hidden by the enormous buildings. We were suddenly in a never-ending desert, the road waving up and down countless dunes. We walked and walked. The road ended in a spot where the sand devoured it, so we stepped off the shards of road onto golden sand. I looked back at the city but the buildings and the winding road were gone, only sand.

The sand was soft and it cushioned our feet as we walked. Looking back again, footprints with no beginning were all I could see. Lisa still danced as she led me by the hand, her dress and hair whirling in the wind. Up ahead, the sand rippled and waved in all directions, suddenly becoming water.

We reached the water and waves crashed in a cascade of white bubbles against the sand at our feet, the white water matching Lisa's dress. She stopped and faced me, the water rising higher and higher, making more and more of her blend with it. Lisa held both my hands and kissed them. She was so beautiful, like a goddess framed in white. Smiling and turning toward the water, she let go of my hands and stepped away from me. The water swirled around her, swallowing her whole. I stood alone on the beach, the waves licking my feet.

Chapter 19

I opened my eyes, wide awake and cold. Only my left hand and jaw were warm. Warmed by somebody's hands. I turned expecting to see Lisa but found Amy sitting beside me on the bed. For a second I didn't know where I was but the panic faded when Amy spoke: "You had a nightmare. Or I guess a daymare. Are you okay?"

"Yeah, it just felt so real."

"What was it about?"

"Lisa."

"It probably was real."

"How do you mean?"

"She was probably saying goodbye."

"You think so. That happens?"

"Never to me but I've heard of it." She took her hand from my jaw and wiped my forehead with a damp cloth.

"Is that water?"

"It's sweat. You were on fire and dripping like a fat man in a sauna."

I chuckled and said, "How long have you been here?"

"About ten minutes. I kept calling to see if you were okay, but you never answered so I just came over."

"How'd you get in?"

"Your door was unlocked and—"

"It was?"

"Yeah. And a nice lady let me in at the front."

She stood up and dropped the cloth on the coffee table. "No work today?"

"I quit."

"Good. Are you hungry?"

"Yeah, or thirsty. I can't tell."

"You should eat something. You'll feel better."

"What time is it?"

"Eleven. When did you eat last?"

"I don't know. Waffles at your place I guess."

"Jesus! I'll make you something."

She stood up and went to the kitchen. I didn't move. I just stared at the ceiling and listened to kitchen sounds clatter through my apartment. When I finally got up and plopped down on the couch in the living room, Amy came out of the kitchen carrying a plate and a glass of orange juice. She put the plate on the table and brought the juice over to me.

"Sit up."

I took the juice and ended up chugging it. Amy took the empty glass and went back into the kitchen. When I sat down at the table, the most delicious looking sandwich greeted me. I wanted to introduce myself to it and take a picture. Amy came back with a refill.

"This looks too good to eat."

"Just eat it."

She went back into the kitchen while I stuffed my face. It felt as if someone was stabbing me in the jaw every time I took a bite but I was too hungry to stop. The food and juice made me feel better than I had in days.

Maybe I had caught something at the hospital. Some disease that's working its way into my bones. Something that made me pass out last night.

"I fainted last night," I said when I'd finished. Amy poked her head around the corner. "And I've felt like throwing up for days. Maybe I should go to a doctor."

She sat down beside me. "It's probably stress and not eating." Amy gently turned my head to the side with her hand. "If you go, it should be to have your jaw checked out. Do you want some ice for it?"

"No, it's fine."

"Mercy do that?"

"Yeah. But I deserved it."

"What happened last night?"

"He hit me because he couldn't go through with it."

Amy furrowed her brow as if trying to read my mind. "He made you do it?"

"He didn't make me do anything. I did it for her."

She sat back and looked stunned. "So I guess you met with her before."

"I did. I saw her parents too. And met her best friend."

"What were they like?"

"Normal." I could see Simone's dull smile. Lisa's parents with their arms around each other. "Sad. Tired."

"And Lisa?"

I tried to picture Lisa but couldn't distinguish her from the vision in my dreams, the figure in the hospital bed, and the person in the videos on Mercy's phone. "She was ah ... she was ready."

"Were you?"

"I'm still not."

"Well, I'm proud of you. Not many people could have done that, for someone they don't know."

No one had ever told me they were proud of me before. The sentiment eased the pain in my jaw. It made me feel happy to be me as if suddenly I had permission.

"Thanks."

"You're welcome." She smiled and said, "So, what now?"

I glanced around my messy apartment, thought of the heap of dirty dishes in the kitchen, and asked Amy if she'd help me clean.

"I've already started the dishes," she said, standing up and moving back toward the sink.

"Thanks. I don't think I could have done them."

"No problem. You just worry about the rest of the place."

"Wait a sec. Sit down," I said, remembering how she'd blown all of her student loan money on her ex-boyfriend's startup, how I had scolded her like a child.

She came back over to the table and stood beside me.

"How did your meeting go with the Dean?"

"Oh, fine I guess. I'm not expelled so that's good. But they're giving me a zero on the assignment."

"That sucks. But it could have been a lot worse."

"Yeah, it was pretty scary sitting in that big room, getting grilled by all of those important-looking people.

They could have expelled me." She stared out the window for a moment.

"Hey," I said, getting her attention, "sorry about yesterday."

"You don't have to be sorry," she said, sitting down. "You were right. It was stupid to sell that stuff and even stupider to invest in a startup with borrowed money."

"Are you going to ask Mum and Dad for money?"

"Maybe. I don't know. I thought I'd just sell fifteen more discs, you know. Just enough to get me through this semester."

Panic crept onto her face. She'd been able to keep it at bay with that fifteen hundred she made so easily, but she needed a lot more.

"Here," I said, "pulling out my phone, launching my bank app, and typing in her email address. "I can give you a thousand."

"What? No." She stood up and grabbed for my phone.

I pulled away from her hands and confirmed the transfer. "Yes. It's already done."

"But you don't even have a job anymore."

"It doesn't matter. Help me clean this place and we'll call it even."

"There's no way there's a thousand bucks worth of cleaning here."

"Are you kidding? I'd pay you that just to do the dishes."

She looked at me for a moment, her expression one of pride and shame. "Seriously though, I can't accept it."

"If it makes you feel any better about it, think of it as back pay for all the Christmas and birthday presents I didn't get you over the years."

"That's silly."

"Just take it. I want to help."

She stood up, looking relieved. "Well, let's clean and then talk about it later."

I nodded, and she went to the sink.

"Would anyone rat you out to the university for selling the program?"

She looked at me, her mouth agape, her hands submerged in soapy water. "I don't think so."

"You were lucky with the plagiarism thing. If you get caught selling pirated versions of software that the university sells and requires their students to have, you'll get expelled and maybe charged."

"I know," she said, nodding and looking down into the murky water that was turning her fingertips into prunes. "It was just such easy money."

"Forget about it. Just get a job and enjoy the fact that you can say you're working towards a degree and that you don't have to check that criminal record box."

"You're right." She washed the dishes slowly at first —her mind obviously trying to come to terms with what she should do—then she sped up.

I cleaned everything up off the floors and grabbed the broom. As I swept and mopped and tidied, the apartment began to feel hollow, like someone else's place; it felt as if I was moving out, and suddenly I wished I was. I couldn't live there anymore, drive those same streets, pass my old job, maybe run into Kurt or Lisa's parents or Mercy. No. The stuff, the apartment, the neighbourhood, the city … it had to go. I had to go.

I ran into the kitchen holding the old, flattened boxes I had used to moved in. Amy was putting clean dishes into the cupboards. "Stop," I said, dropping the boxes and assembling one. "Put them in here."

"What? Why?"

"I'm leaving. All this stuff has to go."

"What do you mean you're leaving?"

"I can't stay here. Not anymore. I have to go."

"Where?"

"It doesn't matter. Just help me pack, okay."

"Okay. But what are you going to do with all this stuff?"

"I don't know." I thought about storage and knew it was a waste of money, thought about lighting a match and walking away. Then the words just came out without any effort or thought: "It's yours. It's all yours. Keep what you want. Sell what you can."

"Wait. No. You just gave me a thousand dollars that I can't accept."

"How much do you owe again?" I asked.

She looked down at the floor and said nothing.

"It's yours." I walked back into the bedroom to start packing up. I knew exactly what I needed—about one percent of what I owned—and what I didn't— practically everything. Glancing around for my duffle bag, I realized that the kitchen was silent. Amy must have been standing there stupefied. "I think there are some newspapers in the recycle bin in the storage room," I called back into the kitchen. "You can use them to wrap the glass stuff." I stood still until I heard the noise of glass on glass begin reverberating through the apartment.

The first thing I filled was my duffle bag: a fraction of my wardrobe—the clothes I actually wore—shoes, my sleeping bag, full bathroom kit, and my two-year-old, unused passport shoved into one of the side pockets. I created a new backup of my computer on my external hard drive and put the little black box containing my entire digital life into my bag. I created a new user account called AMY, logged out of mine and into it. From there, I highlighted my account and clicked DELETE.

"Are you sure you want to delete the user account 'FelixFelix'?" it asked.

I chose delete home folder and let the cursor hover over the DELETE ACCOUNT button for a moment.

It's not really clutter.

It's digital clutter. You don't need it.

But all my stuff?

What do you have on there that's so important?

All my stuff.

It's on the hard drive anyway.

You're right.

And you don't need any of it.

You're right.

I clicked on the DELETE ACCOUNT button and watched the computer process the request for several minutes before the account, my account, disappeared. I sighed and felt lighter.

The duffle bag went by the front door when full, and then I boxed and bagged the rest of my apartment. Two hours later, my entire life was packed and stacked in the living room. Me and Amy stood side by side, staring at the pile.

"Can you deal with this stuff?" I said, my voice echoing off the walls and empty corners of the apartment. The pile of junk clung to my neck like a noose, and only now with it piled in one room did it start to loosen its grip and reveal its penchant for asphyxiation.

"Are you sure?" Amy said.

"It's yours." I looked at the computer box and said, "If you sell the computer, don't accept less than twelve hundred."

"I can't take your computer."

"Take it. You need it more than me."

"What about all your stuff?"

"I deleted it. There's only a new account with your name on it."

"Wow, you deleted it. How'd that feel?"

"Pretty good actually."

We stared at the pile for a moment, the hum of the refrigerator the only sound in the apartment.

"When are you planning on leaving?" Amy said.

"How about now? Can you drive me to the airport?"

"What? Now?"

I nodded.

"Yeah, sure. But, what about your landlord?"

I'd forgotten about her, but she lived three doors down, so I walked down the hall and knocked on her door. I heard a cat meowing before she answered the door in her housecoat, the straps of her nude-coloured bra visible, her hair matted from sleep and neglect, her hairless cat in her arms. I could smell cat piss. The litter box must have been near the entrance. The smell made me think of what Lisa had said about that basilica in Turkey. I wondered if that was Lisa saying goodbye again.

"Oh hey, honey. What's up? I'm just in the middle of my shows," she said, readjusting her housecoat to hide her bra.

"I'm sorry to do this to you but I'm moving out."

"Oh, okay, fine. Ah … When?"

"Now."

"Is everything all right. Are you in—"

"Everything's fine. My sister will be doing the walk through with you. The place is clean and my stuff will be gone in a few days."

"Okay, hon. Just leave her number inside the apartment for me so I have someone to give the damage deposit to." The cat began to struggle for freedom.

"That's great. Thanks."

"Don't mention it, dear. I gotta go. Mr. Wiggles is getting antsy. You take care, okay," she said, shutting her door.

"You too."

"That was easy," I said while stepping back into my place.

Amy was surveying all my former possessions.

"Do whatever you want with it."

It seemed like someone else's stuff sitting there now.

"What did she say?"

"Take care."

Amy nodded. "Cool landlord."

"Can you be here for the walk through?"

"Sure."

"Cool. Here's her info," I said, messaging the contact to Amy. I felt restless standing there; I needed to leave. "Can we go?" I said, stepping out into the hallway.

I left the apartment without checking the stove, without checking the door after I'd turned the key in the lock. I just left.

At the car, I held out the keys to Amy. "You can have this too."

She hesitated before taking them. "Your car? Are you turning into a Buddhist? Jesus, Felix. I can't take this too."

"It's a piece of crap anyway, and I don't need it anymore."

"How about I take care of it for you while you're gone?"

"If you sell it and all that stuff up there, you might be close to that ten grand you lost," I said.

She gazed at the car, her eyes watering, her lower lip quivering a little like it used to when she was little and on the verge of crying.

"Catch," I said before tossing her the keys.

She caught them, took a deep breath, smiled at me, and then got into the driver's seat.

Chapter 20

On the way to the airport, I got Amy to stop at the café. Wanting to see the barista again but having no idea what I'd say to her, I ran inside. A guy was behind the bar. I thought of the girl with her tattoo and pierced button. I would've asked to see her tattoo, told her it was beautiful, that she was beautiful, and left. But instead, I got a latte for Amy and walked out.

We drove to the airport in silence. It was a calm silence, ringing with the racket of thought. I kept rubbing my jaw and seeing Lisa's face. My phone began vibrating. I pulled it out of my pocket to see Mercy's name. The palm-sized computer started to burn my hand as I looked at it. I ignored the call and flipped through my contacts to find Simone's number.

"Do you have a pen?" I asked.

"A pen?" Amy said. "What year is it?"

Reaching into the glovebox, I found a pen, the simplicity of the device making me giggle. I also found an old receipt with faded ink to write on. I copied Simone's phone number onto the paper and then reset my phone. Pressing ERASE made me feel even lighter, but Mercy would still be able to call after the phone restarted.

"Can I borrow one of your earrings?" I asked Amy.

"What for?"

"I can hold the steering wheel if you need help while taking it out."

With one hand, she fiddled with an earring until it came out. After handing it to me, she kept looking over to see what I was going to do with it.

I used it to pop out the sim card in my phone. I gave her back her earring, snapped the little piece of plastic in half, rolled down the window, and tossed it.

"What are you doing?"

"I'm not sure."

The phone still felt hot, so I held it out the window. Gripping it tight at first, the phone grew hotter, but as I relaxed my grip, the air began cooling my palm. The looser the grip, the cooler my hand. Then the phone fell. I heard the faint thud of it hitting the road. After that, no ringing, no vibrating.

"Did you just drop your phone?" Amy said, a panicked expression on her face.

I turned to her, laughing, and said, "I guess I did." I looked back but couldn't see it.

"That was stupid," she said, sounding just like Mum. "I could have sold it for a few hundred bucks."

Her face flushed a little, and she shook her head as she spoke.

"Don't get greedy. I've given you everything else I own."

She glanced at me, her face softening with embarrassment. "Sorry."

"Hey," I said. "I just realized that I don't know your number. What is it? I should probably write it down and try to memorize it." She told it to me, and I wrote her name and number beneath Simone's before folding the receipt and slipping it into my pocket.

Outside departures, I thanked Amy and apologized for dumping so much on her. "I just can't deal with all that shit now," I said.

"Don't worry about it. You're helping me out in the most amazing way. I can't … I'm sorry I was so stupid."

"Don't say that. You made a mistake. It happens. Just don't make it again."

We stood staring at each other for a few seconds. I wanted her to come with me, but knew she couldn't and that I needed to go alone. "I should go."

She laughed. "Where?"

"I have no idea. But I'll call you when I get there."

"How? You don't have a phone anymore."

"Oh, yeah." The idea of not having a phone made me chuckle. "I'll use a pay phone. Wait, do they even exist anymore?"

"I think so. Besides, there are computer stores with free wifi," she said, smirking.

"Funny," I said.

"Don't worry about Mum and Dad. I'll take care of them."

"I don't care what you tell them. Tell them whatever you want. No, tell them the truth. Tell them I had to get away for a while. And if Mercy asks, tell him too."

"I will."

"Well, …" I looked down at my duffle bag and shook it just to feel the new weight of my life—it was light, almost nonexistent.

Amy hugged me. I dropped my bag and squeezed back with both arms. We spoke over each other's shoulders.

"Don't do anything stupid."

"You mean stupider than this?"

"This is just something you have to do."

"I guess. Amy I—"

"I know. Me too." She squeezed me harder. "Thank you, Felix. Thank you for helping me and not judging me and just …" she sniffed back tears. "And just being there for me."

"If I could do more, I would."

"I know. Me too."

It was the longest hug I'd ever had, and I never wanted to let go. When we did finally pull away, we were both crying and smiling, wiping our eyes with our hands. Then I turned, grabbed my bag, and waved before stepping through the huge rotating glass doors of the airport.

Chapter 21

As I sat waiting at my departure gate, three twenty-something women, carrying backpacks that looked far too big for them, staggered down the walkway; I couldn't hear what they were saying but they laughed like little girls at recess; one laughed so hard she had to hold onto her friend's arm to keep from falling over. The other two hunched over and gasped for air while walking past where I sat. I couldn't help smiling and chuckling to myself while watching them.

I pulled the piece of paper, with phone numbers on it, from my pocket. Brushing my finger over Simone's digits, picturing her lips, longing to hear her voice, I reached for my phone only to find an empty pocket. I felt a moment of panic before remembering that the phone was still on the highway, still on its way to the airport. I glanced around for a pay phone. Seeing none, I felt relieved. I ripped the paper in half to separate the phone numbers, putting Amy's info back in my pocket, and crumpling up Simone's before tossing it into the garbage beside me.

I'll never be able to call Lisa's best friend, to lie to her every time we talk.

What would you talk about and who would you think of the entire time?

Lisa.

For a second I wanted to reach into the garbage to retrieve the piece of old receipt paper her number was on, but it was where it belonged. Instead, I again reached for a phone that wasn't there and snickered at the now useless habit I'd have to break. I fingered the little coin pocket of my jeans only to find it empty, no migraine pills. I had used them all up and forgotten to replenish the supply. I had actually forgotten to pack painkillers altogether.

At that moment, I realized my head didn't ache. My jaw radiated heat across the side of my face but there wasn't any pain. I felt tranquil, as if I were experiencing the aftermath of a hangover—throbbing hurt converting to a tingly numbness that seemed to turn the world I watched into a projection on a movie screen and the sounds I heard into an accompanying audio track emanating from a ubiquitous surround-sound system. I watched, listened, and interlaced my fingers on my lap to keep them still, to keep them from reaching into my pocket in search of a nonexistent phone.

As I sat there, waiting for a plane I was extremely early for, watching the gears of the airport spinning and grinding, my thumbs started to twiddle.